SCHIZOPHRENIC'S SPACE JOURNEY

By: Darren & Dianne Aspden

Edited by Austin Mardon

Golden Meteorite Press
Edmonton

A Golden Meteorite Press Book.

Published by Golden Meteorite Press.

Golden Meteorite Press.
Post Office Box 1223, Station Main,
Edmonton, Alberta, Canada. T5B 2W4

ISBN 978-1-897472-04-0

Library and Archives Canada Cataloguing in Publication:

Aspden, Darren, 1961-
   Schizophrenic's space journey / Darren & Diane Aspden.

ISBN 978-1-897472-04-0

   I. Aspden, Diane, 1955- II. Title.

PS8601.S597S35 2008   C813'.6
C2008-902621-7

Dedication

To both of our mothers,

Acknowledgements:

We wish to thank our families for their support and the editorial staff at Golden Meteorite Press for getting this book to publication. We also want to thank each other for our mutual support during the writing and production of this book.

Prologue

After she prayed that God would protect mother, father, chaldra and all the Humans from the Naproxians she went outside the church and ran into a man named Odin.

Smiling more then heavenly father would bide him. Odin recomposed himself, looked at this mystic lady and saw more then his senses could comprehend, what he saw was a Christian warrior woman in plain attire. He had to get to know her on a personal basis, to feel like a gentleman as he took her to a dance. Yet he promised God that he would not violate this special and mysterious creature he was confronted with.

Odin was thinking only the bible cherished the thought of unicorns in order to remember the times before the flood, the way Heather looked she was, indeed, like a Unicorn, because she was so unordinary.

Odin started to chuckle as he stared at Heather. Heather smiled back at Odin. Then shivers went down Odin's spine as he imagined her dressed in royal attire. It may be a better idea to treat her ordinary he thought.

Rex, a merchant from Ireland watched Odin and Heather looking at each other. Odin was the son of a wealthy artist and Heather, a princess. He knew both of their parents and it was more the possible that they would make a perfect match. He knew that Heather excelled at peaceful school and would make a perfect wife for any man.

Nearby, Oda, a priest of sorcery, felt both fear and hope when he looked into his crystal ball. He observed a war thousands of years ago between their between their ancestors before they signed a peace treaty. If these two were to get married, it would put the worlds at peace except for the menace of the Naproxians. The Oda had an itch and scratched it. Then Oda and Rex looked at each other, nodded and

Oda closed his eyes. He put his long lonely cloak on and headed in the direction of the setting sun.

Chapter 1:

"Within Westmore Land in Great Britain in the Year of 1300"

Heather both blinked and gurgled toward her mother Grace, from a thick blanket folded on a dirt floor. They resided in a fine log cabin located in a magical place within Westmore Land.

"I feel so blessed that our relatives relocated us to this beautiful planet Heather, it resembled royalty." Grace whispered to her sensitive baby.

"I am preparing Heather's healthy supper meal," John interrupted Grace. The formula contained crushed wheat, half goat's milk and the other half cow's milk.

The cabin servant, Chalda, went over to the plump, smiling and healthy child then she sang out a lullaby, while John spooned supper into Heather's mouth:

"Oh little child who came here from the stars, I dream good fortune to all that arrived here from afar."

"That was such a nice lullaby Chalda, yes our relatives saved us from the Naproxion's 5 light years form this Earth planet," blessed Grace.

The Naproxians used loving races as slaves and sexual objects on a labor planet referred to as the Naprox Trade Planet.

Chalda remembered, as a child, how the Naproxians used her and those memories caused a feeling of fear to ripple thoughout her body.

"Westmore Land is the perfect niche to raise a bumbling child as our neighbors work together as a community, right John?" Chalda asked.

"They certainly regard us as member of their family," John replied.

"I am going to add a little nature to the inside of our home by putting these tulips Jack gave us for Easter, into a vase," commented Grace.

On the basin, one tulip was dead. Grace set it by the cabin door. Little Heather crawled over to the dead flower and picked it up. This event was special as all were silent and watched Heather. A team trickled down Heather's left cheek when she examined the dead plant. Grace went over to Heather, with a cloth, and wiped the single tear off Heather's cheek.

"Such a sensitive little one, just like your Aunt Margaret was, it's a gift child."

Heather looked up to her mother, dropped the flower and held out her hands to be picked up. This moment was sacred and one could not hear anything. Heather hid her face in the shoulder of her mother.

"There, there child," Grace nurtured. After a few more moments, Heather fell fast asleep and Mom put her into bed.

The next day was Easter Sunday and John planned out church and a picnic for everyone. They all hugged and went to bed except Grace who took her candle and kneeled down beside Heather and said a prayer:

"Now I lay me down to sleep. I pray the lord my soul to keep. If I shall die before I wake, then take my soul for heaven's sake."

John put on his work clothing, at the crack of dawn, on Easter morning. He fed 12 sheep, 2 goats, 1 cow, 20 chickens and 5 ducks. He also both prepared the horses and killed and gutted a chicken for the picnic. Then he woke all up for his special Easter day. All of the adults helped pack the picnic basket and they mounted their horses and headed toward the Christian Church.

When they arrived at the church, they met up with their good friend Rex and other member of the community such as: The Smith family, the Brown family and, of course, their minister...Mr. Right. Some unknown strays also entered the church and took their respectable seats on the spruce benches.

Mr. Right stood in front of the congregation as he spoke:

"I sincerely welcome all you Christians into the Church representing God. My intention today is to reinforce Christ's most important message:"

"You should love thy neighbor as you love either yourself or your family!"

And then the minister told the church to refer to 'Psalm 150':

"Praise ye the Lord, Praise God in his sanctuary: praise him in the firmament of his power. Praise him for his mighty acts: Praise him according to his excellent greatness. Praise him with the sound of the trumpet: Praise him with the psaltery and harp. Praise him with the timbrel and dance: Praise him with stringed instruments and organs.

The minister stood in silence as an "angel like" blond woman entered with a golden harp singing this song:

"Jesus loves me yes I know for the bible tells me so. Little ones he specially adores. Jesus loves me even more. Yes, Jesus loves me! Yes, Jesus loves me! Yes, Jesus loves me! For the bible tells me so."

She then exited the church and the minister took over and said, "The service has ended and you are all blessed by: God the Father! God the Son! And God the Holy Spirit! Please go in peace and serve each other."

All the members of the congregation met each other outside. They shook hands, talked and then left bidding each "Happy Easter!" John's family and servant mounted their horses in order to find a spot for the picnic. They chase a spot in a barley field that grew around a mountain with a shiny creek running through the barley field into the mountain. The sun was bright and located at the noon hour position. They laid out a large blanket near the creek for their picnic.

Heather stared at the mountain and squinted her eyes in wonder. Grace noticed her daughter's reaction to the mountain and instructed her, "Mountain, beautiful mountain." As Heather stared at the mountain she became hungry and her belly made a sound for food.

"The fresh air and the sight of the mountain has caused an appetite," her mother remarked. So, her mother went over to the picnic basket and took out her food. Then she fed spoonfuls of food into her as fast as she swallowed each.

John was standing next to his wife and baby looking at the Creek and made the remark, "Next time we come here I will try my luck at fishing."

"You are the best when it comes to fishing!" said Chalda.

"John I am hungry and my stomach can't wait until you get around to starting a fire and roasting the chicken, so I am going to help myself to potato salad," Grace said in one breath.

"Go right ahead and I will gather wood for the fire!"

While John was gone from the rest of them, some wild dogs came into sight. They salivated as they looked at Heather. Then Chaldra saw the dogs and yelled out, "My God! Wild dogs, where is John?" she exclaimed.

"He has went for wood!" said Grace.

The wild dogs with saliva running down their jaws moved slowly toward them. Grace and Chaldra never considered their own safety, but ran to Heather and huddled each ones body around her and prayed to God.

"Dear heavenly father if the dogs attack please let them take us and protect Heather, Amen," Grace prayed with mercy.

Both Grace and Chaldra were very afraid as the dogs moved in closer and closer. Then the dogs turned around and ran away. The looked at the side of the Creek, and saw Rex.

"You ladies okay?" Rex asked.

"Rex, thank God," replied Grace.

"Those dogs are strays. They have scared folk before. All one has to do is knock a couple of rocks together like these, and they will run away," explained Rex.

"We are so grateful Rex. Will you join us for lunch?" asked Grace.

"Thank ya for the invitation, Mam, but unfortunately I have an important errand to run for Mr. Good."

"However, ask John as to whether or not it's possible to trade some blankets and spices for a few sheep?" Rex asked.

"I am quite certain that John will make you a deal. Just come by some time," Grace assured.

"Look forward to seeing ya all again and if those strays bother you, just knock a couple of rocks together."

"Bye Rex," Grace and Chaldra yelled simultaneously. "Take care!"

Within the next couple of moments, John returned to the picnic site with his arms full of wood.

"I heard you ladies yell, so I ran back as fast as possible with the wood."

"We were attacked by wild dogs, but fortunately Rex came by and scared them off," Grace explained.

"Also he mentioned trading some of his goods for a couple of sheep."

"Grace, thank God you are okay. I feel so bad leaving all three of you alone in the wild."

Chaldra realized how embarrassed John was and in order to make him feel better referred to faith.

"John, God has his ways of looking out for his people!"

John still felt bad as he looked at innocent Heather.

"Wintin myself I feel so sorry for what happened," John blushed.

John then started up the fire and gathered up choice branches to roast the chicken on. It was dawn by the time they finished eating. So they cleaned up, loaded up their horses and rode back to the cabin.

After reaching home safely, the horses were unloaded, Heather was put to bed as Grace prayed by her blanket:

"Dear God, thank you for sending Rex to scare off those wild dogs and especially thank you that my Heather is safe, amen."

Shortly after the prayer the rest of them got ready for bed. They all hugged before blowing out the candle as they went to bed, that evening.

Chapter II

Heather grew up into a 13 year old lady. As she was growing both Grace and Chaldra taught her about herbal medicine and John instructed her as to how to take care of livestock. She also learned the basics in history, math and English study. Of all the many events Heather experienced one was specially unusual. It happened during a fishing trip with her father:

"The first thing to remember dear, before fishing, is to bait your hook with a worm." John explained, "next throw the hook into the water and wait for a fish to strike." As the two of them waited by the Creek, Heather felt that the poor fish must feel pain with a hook in its mouth and then in the next moment John yelled, "I have had a bite Heather!"

He gripped his rod and began to bring the fish into shore. The fish jumped and twisted before it was finally brought onto the land. Heather estimated from math that the brook trout was about 5 pounds. She made this guess based on the math her parents taught her.

John held up the brook trout and asked Heather, "What do you think?"

"About 5 pounds."

"Not a bad guess."

John told Heather to watch him gut and filet the fish.

"I can't watch you do it," Heather said. Then she went running behind their black horse. Only then did John understand that within Heather was still a girl.

It was fun catching the fish but the rest of the operation did not appeal to her at this point in time. Her father felt quite amused by Heather's response. In the future Heather chose to stay home with Chaldra and her mother rather then to go fishing.

Mother continued to teach Heather herbal medicine, knitting and cooking, however had a hard time understanding new abilities that were psychic and she had a sensitivity towards plants and animals.

Her questions about these things would be answered in the near future when she moved into "Peaceful School." It was hard on her mother who realized soon Heather would be a young lady, leave home and attend "Peaceful School." Her love for her daughter, however deep, must not interfere with her leaving in order to learn the art of peace she realized. The arrangements were already being made for the journey, which her father would make with her to the "Peaceful School" in Wishmore Territories.

Heather started to cry a little when the say arrived for the journey. She helped her mother pack some belongings and they held arms and smiled at each other. John and Heather loaded and mounted the horses and Grace hid them a safe journey.

For safety they would travel by day and sleep by fire at night. He always would keep a close eye on her and the horses. She loved her father very much and when she started 'Peaceful School" would miss each other.

They were both exhausted at the end of the day. John tied the horses to an old oak tree, started a fire and laid out blankets not far from the fire. They were happy from traveling through such beautiful country.

John stared at his daughter as she fell asleep. His memory remembered her at two years old when the single tear rolled down her blushed cheek as she held the dead flower. The he went over to her as she was sleeping and said a prayer," Now I lay me down to sleep, I pray the Lord my soul to keep If I shall die before I wake, then take my soul for heaven's sake. I also pray for your "Angels" to watch not only us as we journey to 'Peaceful School' but for the safety of Grace and Chandra at the cabin."

Perhaps, John thought, it was a miracle from the eternal 'God' that we are all on such a peaceful and loving planet called Earth, here perhaps love may be found anywhere.

The next moment John's expression changed at the memory of the Naproxians. What would they do, if or when, they found Earth. He remembered his parents as slaves to these creatures, that felt no mercy, killed on a whim and behaved like robotic machines. After that thought John laid down beside Heather and had a restless sleep.

The morning sun woke up John but Heather was only half awake. He looked at her and felt good that soon she would start "Peaceful School." One day she would learn the truth that she is a princess from the stars. As he stared at her, he though of men that may tempt her on a sexual basis as she becomes more mature. It was his hope that when that time comes she would find a loving and Christian man. He should be sincere, God fearing and live a life like our Saviour Jesus Christ.

"Will you talk a moment dear?" He lightly touched Heather's arm to wake her up.

She yawned, "good morning father, what's up?"

"Heather, I just wanted to give you some fatherly advice."

"What daddy?"

"It is just that you are becoming very attractive and I fear some non-Christian man in the future may take advantage of you on a sexual basis....just be sure you love your choice Heather," her dad advised.

"Don't worry Dad he will have to be equal or better than you."

John and Heather had breakfast, mounted their horses and continued their journey to "Peaceful School."

"Help me with these reins a bit Heather. This horse needs a little more breathing room."

Heather held the horse's head back and John readjusted its reins.

"Thanks Heather, mount your horse and we will be on our way."

"I am looking forward to the next crossing Heather, it is called the remarkable 'Valley of Passion.'"

As they looked into the deep valley, Heather's eyes widened at the sight. The depth of the valley seemed endless and both of the sides of it were covered with green flora.

Then Heather's horse accidentally hit a loose rock on the trail. The rock fell into the valley and hit other rocks, causing rumbling sounds as the rocks descended into the valley. The next moment, Heather's horse jumped to the left of the cliff and Heather lost control of the horse. Her father quickly pulled his horse in front of hers and both horses came to a halt.

"Your horse got a little jumpy Heather, do your best to watch out for rocks on the trail, okay?"

"Okay, Dad, it will not happen again."

She felt both foolish and like a child again. Yes, she realized, she had so much yet to learn

Heather did not conceive of any danger as they continued on their way. However, through experience her father secretly knew that possibilities of danger existed. As they continued God poured out his Holy Spirit on them and Heather's baby blue eyes sparkled.

John wondered with a heart full of love, as to whether or not they had sheltered Heather too much regarding some of the evils possible within the world. Then he changed his mind and thought, "it's a remarkable world, isn't it?"

Heather enjoyed their pilgrimage on their way to "Peaceful School" as they went through the trails, trees and wild flowers. It was beautiful to be beside Mother Nature and, more so, the chance to get so close to and know her father, on a personal basis.

They approached a man made bridge which was about 50 yards from the "Peaceful School."

"Not far now Heather, it is that giant fortress just straight ahead, do you see it?"

"Amazing, father, it looks so wonderful!"

As they arrived to the front gate and pulled their horses to a halt, Heather could feel her heart beating with excitement. She took a deep, fresh breath of air, let it out slowly as her father dismounted his horse and he went to the huge gate and announced their arrival through a message hole.

The huge gate opened up, a moment of silence everywhere and Heather just stared. It was even more than she had dreamed of. A man in a purple Christian robe stepped out of the "peaceful school's" gate and looked at them.

"God bless you both and I am gratified that your journey was safe. Please enter," the minister invited.

"Thank you," replied John.

John and Heather walked their horsed through the gate in the 'peaceful school' led by the minister and he closed the doors behind them. The minister took their horses to a stable and then led Heather and John to the 'eatery' at which time the staff brought them fresh fruit and water. The minister sat on a bench in front of them.

"How was the trip?" he asked.

"It was safe," replied John.

"It was beautiful, fund and wonderful!" inserted Heather.

"After your refreshments, I will take you on a tour," said the minister.

The tour took about an hour and a half. The last stop was the sleeping quarters. Half were reserved for young men, the other half for young women. The minister told John to stay the night and told him that his horses would be watered and fed. John replied that he would only stay one night because he was responsible for Grace and Chaldra at the cabin. They both agreed. Later, after supper, everyone went to bed.

A big bell rang in the morning, everyone heard grace and ate a healthy breakfast. After breakfast Minister Wise led John, Heather, and the horses to the massive gates and opened them.

Heather looked into her Dad's eyes and momentarily lost her excitement about the school and only thought about Mom, Dad and Chaldra. A flood of good memories flooded her mind as her imagination pictured each one of them. Three or four tears rolled down her cheek while she looked into her father's eyes.

"Bye father, I love you and I love mom and Chaldra also."

Then she ran to her Dad and wrapped her arms around his waist. He gently put his arms around her too.

"I am so proud of you, Heather and I love you very much."

After hugging and tears were over, John went over to his horse and handed the spare horse to Heather as a gift. He bid farewell and headed home to the log cabin.

Chapter 3

The next day the sun rose giving off crisp rays of sunlight. Ernie, a fat man with a bald head and shaved face, walked over to the hanging bell rope, grabbed it with his small, fat fingers and pulled down on it three times. A loud 'dong, dong, dong' sound shimmered from the bell.

"That's a good sound!" Ernie said.

Within the school everybody woke up. The men and women all washed their faces and hands in a water basin. The men also had a clean shave.

Next everyone entered 'The Eatery' but before anyone tasted the fruit and porridge or drank the fruit juice, the minister entered the room. On his way to the head of the table he shook hands with some of the students. The minister wore a robe with shiny yellow stars on it, and also he wore a giant brown cross around this neck. When he reached the head of the table he spoke with a firm voice, "we are blessed to have the best of everything here. Heavenly Father, we give thanks for the food we are about to receive, Amen."

After breakfast was done the program coordinator came in. She wore a brown robe, was short and had red hair. She looked at everyone and then when they were silent began to speak, "my name is Jill and if anyone has any questions or complaints regarding their program then they must report to me."

Jill assigned each student to a house. Heather was assigned to the 'Green House.' The other houses were called, "The Red House," "The Black House," and "The Yellow House."

Jill then led each house to an assigned faculty. 'The Green House' was assigned to the war zone. Jill wished 'The Green House' luck and then she moved on. Heather marveled at the targets 30 yards from where she stood.

The war zone instructor was well built, had blond hair and blue eyes. His voice sounded both gentle and experienced. He looked at everyone within the 'green house' and began to speak, "you will master three weapons referred to as the cross bow, the bow and arrow, and the shield and sword. My name is Jeff, and in time I will get to know each one of you on a personal basis."

The Jeff carefully picked up the cross bow.

"This weapon is referred to as the cross box, it is used for hunting and to engage a dangerous enemy such as the Naproxians," Jeff explained. "And it has an ancestral song that sounds like this, "
Take the mighty cross box. It may defeat a dangerous foe. How effective it will be. To use against a mighty enemy."

"Does anybody know about the dangerous race referred to as the Naproxian," Jeff quizzed.

Heather remembered what her parents had told her about them when she was younger. So she put up her hand to answer the question.

"Yes, Heather please answer the question."

"They are large, merciless, and without feelings and use human beings as slaves and sex objects."

She recalled the fear in the eyes of her parents as she told Jeff about them.

"The only weakness they have is that they are very attached to their young!" Jeff explained.

The class was both silent and scared as Heather and Jeff talked about the treacherous race.

Next Jeff put down the cross bow and picked up the bow and arrow. "This weapon is referred to as the bow and arrow. It is used for the same purposes as the cross bow, however, it is larger and can not be used in crowded places." Jeff explained. "It also has an ancestral song and it sounds like this, "The bow and arrow. The bow and arrow. I am brave with this weapon. I carry it on the back with me. For any enemy may soon see. The bow and arrow. The bow and arrow. Watch out treacherous enemy."

Jeff looked at the whole 'green house' for any questions but everyone was silent.

"Before we move onto the last weapon, I just wanted to add what can be done to the arrows of this weapon. The tips of the arrows may be dipped into lethal poison!"

Then as Jeff looked at all the student's faces, all he could see was a look of awe on them, and so he continued, "This final weapon is referred to as the sword and shield. It is used in close combat and takes a lot of practice." Jeff smiled. "It also has a song attached to it, "They come big and strong. With my sword I knock them down. When they strike I use my shield. Even the best will soon yield!"

Jeff had finished for the day and told the class to bow their heads in prayer, "Dear heavenly Father, may each member here use these weapons only if it is your will to use them and may your Holy Spirit bless each one of them, amen."

"Class is now dismissed and enjoy the rest of the day, make friends and enjoy the board games."

Within a few days the class was getting quite good at the weapons each was practicing. Heather was quite good with the cross bow and was hitting the bulls eye 90% of the time. An evil spirit entered into a girl named Chris and whispered to her, "Heather is being treated better than you, so you should not like her."

Chris then was not satisfied with her own ability and became very jealous of Heather. Chris both watched and listened when Jeff walked over to Heather and said, "You handle that cross bow like an experienced marksman."

"It takes a lot of concentration and patience and I wish father could see me," responded Heather.

As Jeff watched Heather, he thought of her family's secret, that one day she would be reviled as a princess, from a far away planet referred to as 'Zoraster.' He also, noticed that she was becoming quite beautiful.

After complimenting Heather, Jeff made his rounds to each one of the rest of the students and both complimented and helped them. When he came to Chris, she said, "Heather makes me nervous the way she looks at me and thinks she is better than everyone."

"Remember that special passage in the bible

Chris, 'Those who are first will be last and those who are last will be first.' Just do your best Chris and don't compare yourself to others," Jeff said with a fatherly voice.

It was 2 weeks into the program and most of the students were performing on a satisfactory basis.

Jill came over to the war zone and told all the students to come over to her and sit cross legged in front of her.

"Three days from now is 'Ancestor's Day' and our custom is to feast on wild boar at our supper meal," Jill explained. "Only two groups will be chosen for the hunt from cross bow group. The choices will be announced tomorrow at breakfast."

She nodded at Jeff as she left. Jeff smiled at the class then dismissed them.

The students kept themselves busy talking about their different faculty, playing board games, and making new friends.

Heather was playing a board game called 'Peaceful Retreat' with a young man and Chris saw them having fun. The evil spirit entered Chris and said, "There's that Heather that gets better treatment than you."

"So you think you are better than the rest of us Heather!"

"Are you talking to me Christ?" asked Heather.

"Yes, and one day I will surpass you in everything Heather."

"I like you Chris and would you like a game of 'Peaceful Retreat?"

"No!"

Her attitude not only hurt Heather, but confused her, but Heather remembered that to change anger into love.

"Maybe we can play another time Chris?"

"NO!"

"Chris I know within yourself you are a kind loving person or you would not have been a candidate for 'peaceful school.'

"Good?" "What Good?" ..."Survival!" Chris

yelled.

After that Chris stomped out of the gaming room and went all alone and sat down in front of a weeping willow tree. Then she looked up to the sky and the heavens opened up and a flock of birds of all different kinds flew out and then she heard the voice of God, "Chris, and evil spirit tempted you to turn against Heather. As you hear my voice, remember I love you very much and so do the people at the 'peaceful school.' Repent from your sin and rebuke the devil and I will bless you."

When Chris heard God's voice her heart felt full of 'love,' she felt sleepy and fell asleep in front of the tree. As she slept, she thought about her mother who was both tortured and killed by the Naproxians and her father who still lives a the 'Mountain of Faith' who used most of his savings to bring her to 'peaceful school.' Then the dream went away and she woke up both in tears and feeling a need to be held.

No sooner did she stand up that she saw Heather standing in front of her. Heather had seen her sleeping in front of the 'willow tree' and walked over in order to check on her.

"Why are you crying Chris," Heather asked.

"It was just a dream," replied Chris.

"It must have been a nightmare!"

Heather saw the timid side of Chris and put her long arms around her. Chris also embraced Heather and they both realized that God meant for them to be best friends.

Shortly after the hug of a very special friendship the supper bell rang. So Heather and Chris, feeling rather hungry, went to 'the eatery' to fill their bellies up. Minster Right came out to the head of the table in order to say grace before the meal, "Heavenly Father, we give thanks for the meal we are about to consume tonight. Also may his Holy Spirit fill up each one of us within this room."

Tonight supper consisted of deer steak, mixed vegetables and potatoes. Everyone completely loved eating their healthy meal. After supper, and putting their dishes into the basin everybody just leisured around and talked before bed time.

The next morning the bell rang three times waking everybody up. They all went to 'the eatery' for breakfast. After breakfast was over, Jill came to the front of the table and announced the teams that would be going on the boar hunt, "Listen everyone, the two groups we have carefully picked, to work as teams for the boar hunt for 'Ancestor's Day' are Heather and Chris and Gary and Mike. Jeff will give you the details in class. Let's everybody give them a hand."

Clap! Clap! Clap! Clap!

At the war zone Jeff said, "Heather, Chris, Gary and Mike today we will be leaving 'Peaceful School' in order to learn how to track and hunt."

Jeff gave all four of them smocks, a back pack and hiking foot wear to put on. He taught them how to follow tracks, how to study scat, and how to camouflage themselves. After two hours of intense training all five of them went back to 'peaceful school.' When they finally returned, Jeff said that their class would be extended today because the targets would be changed from 'bull's eyes' to pictures of 'boars' for target practice.

While the war zone hunters were practicing on the boar target, Heather noticed that Chris was having a hard time with her cross bow. She went over to Chris to give her a helping hand.

"Do you mind if I give you a pointer or two as to how to master the cross bow?" Heather asked.

"Of course not, I guess I just can't get the hang of it," replied Chris.

"You hold it firmly onto your shoulder, then you focus the target with your sights, these little things there, once you have your target in sight, then you release the arrow," Heather said firmly, "try it."

"Okay, like this?" asked Chris.

"Exactly," reaffirmed Heather. "Now when you're ready, shoot."

As the arrow left the cross bow this time, it hit the boar target right into the boar's head.

"Very, very good Chris," Heather said kindly.

About an hour and a half later, Chris hitting the target everytime now, Jeff came back into the picture.

"It looks as though you are all prepared for hunting wild boar tomorrow, Heather I noticed the comradeship you showed Chris, and I bless you for it. Everybody put down your heads for prayer, "Lord I thank you for the love I saw in class today as the not so good students helped the good students to become better. Bless you all in the Lord's name, amen."

"It is almost supper time so I dismiss the class and thank you for staying later today. See you in the morning for the wild boar hunt." Jeff ended the day.

About an hour and a half later everybody was made aware that it was supper time.

Ernie, with his fat little fingers, pulled the bell three times:

"Dong!" "Dong!" "Dong!"

He felt good that he had that responsibility and it wasn't that hard, he thought, pulling the bell rope three times a day. The rest of the time he spent watching the students in different faculties.

Ernie was a simple man, although when he was young, he was a prisoner of the Naproxians. They killed his family in front of him and they tortured him on several occasions. He, in a sense, is not only a 'bell ringer' but a war hero. 'Peaceful School' is the only home he has now.

As everybody walked into the 'eatery' for supper, Heather noticed Chris sitting alone and went up to her and asked, "Chris do you mind me joining you for supper."

"Not at all," Chris replied.

They talked about how excited they were to go on their first boar hunt and Christ expressed how good of a teacher Heather was, even better than Jeff, Christ said. Heather truly believed in God now because she realized that only god could have given her such a special friend.

As Chris and Heather talked away they then became quiet as Minister Right entered the room. They both felt very special this time as Minister Right stopped by them and gave them both a giant hug. They wondered as to what they did to deserve that. Then the minister shook hands with a few other students and proceeded to the head of the large table and began to say grace, "As we gather here today, we are reminded that in two days we celebrate 'Ancestor's Day' and we have two brave groups who have been specially picked to hunt wild boar for our evening meal. I bless this food and all of you, in the name of the Father, Son and Holy Spirit. Enjoy your meal, Amen"

Tonight was a different type of meal as everyone was served lamb stew in quite a large wooden bowl. Beside each bowl of stew were two pieces of buttered bread to dip into the stew. Everyone seemed to enjoy this meal more than ever.

"This stew, although more simple than most of our meals is very good," Heather said.

"Ya, I really like it, yummy," Chris replied.

"A little bit of imagination goes a long way," Heather added.

"That's it, one has to use their imagination to get by," Chris said.

"100% that's it!" Agreed Heather.

After supper had ended and as everyone took their wooden bowls and put them into the washing basin a young man named Mark came up to Heather, "Would you like to go for a game of 'peaceful retreat' Heather?"

"Sure thing, can Chris join us?"

"Would you like to Chris?" Heather asked.

"I would love to, but unfortunately I don't know how to play," Chris replied.

"Remember that you thought of me as a better teacher than Jeff," Heather reminded.

"Well then let's all three of us go and play," Chris said.

The three of them: Mark, Heather and Chris went into the 'game room' and played 'peaceful retreat' until sunset and to all three of them, a surprise, Chris was the champion.

Mark, Heather and Chris, without a doubt,

would all become close. Mark's dad is a lumberjack and his mother is a Christian attorney. The both have high standards and raised Mark in such a way as to not only respect others but to treat them as equals.

"Everybody within the Christian community and even those who are not Christian have within them both knowledge and skills and you must always treat them as equals." He could remember his mother telling him, before he fell asleep that night.

Mark was fond of Heather, as a friend, but especially fond of Chris in, such a way, that she resembled his mother Carol. The way in which she was at first the underdog then made a come back as the hero. It was something they both had in common, also, they were both born in October.

It was bed time now and everybody within 'peaceful school' kneeled down beside their bed and did that special Christian Prayer, "Now I lay me down to sleep. I pray the Lord my soul to keep. If I should die before I wake then take my soul for heaven's sake."

After prayer time Heather crawled into bed, snuggled up with the covers and fell asleep dreaming of her mom and dad and all the fond memories about them.

It seemed no longer had everyone drifted off to sleep that the morning bell rang: Dong! Dong! Dong! Dong! And it was breakfast time.

After everyone was served their respectful meal Minister Right, took his usual spot a the head of the table, and began to speak, "Today is a very special day, on the basis, that two teams, 'Heather and Chris' and 'Gary and Mike' are going on their first boar hunt for us to celebrate 'Ancestor's Day' tomorrow. And God bless the food we are about to consume. Amen."

Heather and Chris now sat together during their meals.

"I have never killed anything before and I am a little nervous and excited by the boar hunt," Heather said.

"I haven't neither, but I think Jeff has trained

us well," Chris replied.

Mark walked over to Heather and Chris after they put their dishes into the washing basin.

"Can we have a group hug in order to wish you luck on your boar hunt."

They both looked at Mark and blushed a little. Then they looked at each other.

"A hug can't hurt," Chris said.

"I guess it will be okay," Heather replied.

"Okay," Chris and Heather said at once. They all embraced and Mark proudly put his strong young arms around them and gave them a bear hug.

"Good Luck!" Mark said.

"Thank you," they said.

Heather and Chris headed over to the war zone to meet up with Jeff and get the gear…excreta. They are both very excited and can hardly wait to face the wild boar with the 'cross bow.'

After getting ready Jeff led both teams to the large gates. As they are past the gate Jeff yelled, "be careful and good luck!"

After searching a couple of hours Heather finally finds a clue, "fresh scat and tracks!" She says.

"Whisper and let's follow the tracks," Chris replies.

As they follow the tracks they are full of excitement and fear. Finally just ahead of them they spot the wild boar eating leaves. The boar, also, spots them and out of instinct stops eating and comes running toward them.

"My God, it's attacking us!" exclaims Chris.

"Move behind the trees and load our 'cross bows!'" Yells Heather.

The boar takes its tusk and engages it into Heather's left leg while Chris shoots an arrow into its upper back. The boar drops dead and Heather is in pain. Then Chris brings her first aid kit out of her gear and wraps up Heather's wound.

"You going to be okay, Heather?" Chris asks with concern.

"Ya, I think so. If you can handle carrying the boar over your shoulders, then I can handle walking," Heather explains.

Meanwhile, Gary and Mike kill a boar without incident and are headed back to 'peaceful school.' They arrive back before Heather and Chris. Jeff is at the gate and congratulates them on their kill.

"Thank you. It was easy," Mike said.

"It just stood their and we put a couple of arrow into it," explained Gary.

An hour later, Heather and Chris finally made it back to 'peaceful school' and Jeff opened up the gate for them.

"What happened to you Heather?" Jeff asked.

"The boar attacked and got me with a tusk," Heather said.

"I will carry the boar and Chris help Heather find one of our nurses and get some stitches in that wound, okay?" asked Jeff.

"Okay," answered Chris.

So, Chris helped Heather find a nurse and got four stitches but she was okay.

"You're lucky," the nurse said.

"The stitches were more painful than the tusk," Heather admitted.

"Oh well, you will have a small scar, but it should heal well, just keep it wrapped up dear," the nurse explained. "You are free to go for a bite to eat."

Lunch was over, but Jeff told all four of them to go to the 'eatery' and he would arrange for some food and refreshments. After eating Heather and Chris went for a walk around the grounds, talked and ran into Mark. He noticed that Heather's leg was wrapped up, "What happened Heather?" Mark asked.

"Oh nothing. The wild boar attacked," Heather said bravely.

"Thank God, it only got your leg," Mark said looking concerned.

"I carried the boar all the way home," Chris said.

"Do you two feel like doing anything," Mark asked.

"Lets go over to the willow tree, lay down,

rest and talk before supper time. Chris and I are tired," said Heather.

"Okay," said Mark.

The three of them lay on their backs by the willow tree and talked about their childhood memories, the boar hunt and just about anything. Then Heather and Chris fell asleep and Mark lay there with his eyes closed feeling love for both of them. They were as close as brothers and sisters. All three had become special friends, indeed.

Chapter 4

Heather is eighteen now and has become a master of all the different faculties. It has been five long, hard but cherished years and she is now tall and has a medium frame and very good looking as a woman. Today her Dad will be meeting her to take her home. She is very excited to see her mom and Chaldra too.

The minister went into Heather's room. "Your dad is at the front gate and I am going to take him to the 'eater' for food and drink and fee and water his horse," Minister Wise said.

"May I come?" Heather asked.

"Of course."

At the eatery, Heather met up with her dad and Minister Wise.

"We have a special secret to disclose to you Heather," said Minister Wise.

"What?" asked Heather.

"I think it is better that your father tell you Heather."

"What father?"

"Many years ago your mom and I were Queen and King from a far away planet called 'Zoraster' and you were born a princess. But the evil Naproxians invaded our planet and our family was hidden on Earth," her father explained.

After the refreshments and food Minister Wise said he would be back within a couple of moments. Upon his return he was carrying a medium sized sack.

"This is for you Heather as a parting gift. The sack includes a cross bow, a bow and arrows, sword and shield, a game of 'peaceful retreat' and most important, a Holy Bible." Heather thanked Minister Wise and they all retrieved Heather's and her dad's horse and headed toward the giant gate. This time Heather proudly left her horse a moment and opened up the huge gates. After Heather, her father and the horses went through the gates, and mounted their horses then Minster Wise said a prayer for them both, "God bless Heather and John and keep them protected as they travel back to their cabin in 'Westmore Land' amen."

It was two days into their journey home that Heather was awakened by a loud whistling noise and looked up into the sky and saw a space ship. "Father wake up. Look into the sky," Heather said shaking her father.

"What's wrong Heather?" her father asked with a yawn.

"Look up into the sky, what is that?"

"That Heather is the thing I most feared for the last eighteen years. It's a damn Naproxian surveillance ship."

"We will have to tell Minister Right and send a messenger to warn Minister Wise and the rest of us. Those bastards finally found us, damn!" John exclaimed.

After returning to their cabin in Westmore Land safely, John left Heather with Grace and Chaldra and then rode his horse to Minister Right's church. Upon arriving he knocked at the door of the Minister's house.

"Minister we have trouble," John said after the Minister opened his door.

"What is it son?" asked the Minister.

"The Naproxians have sent a surveillance ships to Earth. We saw it on the way home from 'peaceful school.' We will have to send a messenger out to warn all the people, maybe two or three messengers would be better!" John exclaimed.

"I will send three of my most efficient young men out to warn everyone then!" Minister Good exclaimed. "How's Heather?"

"She has turned into a remarkable woman."

"Good, so you get back to your family, John!" The Minister ordered.

"Yes sir, and take care."

"You too, bye now."

Meanwhile on the Naproxian surveillance ship the two lizard like surveyors and a baby were having a conversation.

"May tech Luway humoh goola dash," said

Lizard A.

[My looks like we found a human colony.]

"Su land de noba nuck," replied Lizard B.

[They will make good slaves.]

"Leb Krock ze yat far," said Lizard A.

[Let's survey this area more.]

"Bango gota mea won," a baby lizard said.

[I want a baby human to bathe me.]

The ship flew over 'peaceful school' and saw the new 13 year old students then they were satisfied that this would be a good area to invade. They turned their ship around and headed back into space to the mother ship.

Meanwhile the three Christian messengers rode from family to family, village to village and all the training schools in order to warn them of a possible invasion.

As one of the messengers came to 'peaceful school,' Minister Wise opened the huge gate, "Hi, I am Minister Wise and who are you?"

"I am Gary, a messenger from Westmore Land"

"What's up?"

"I wanted to report that a Naproxian surveillance ship was spotted by John and Heather.

The minister studied Gary's face a few moments hoping it was a hoax. But after looking directly into Gary's eyes, he could tell, God, he was telling the truth, "I will see to it that all my graduated from the last five years are both armed and put on alert!" Minister Wise exclaimed. "Please let me feed your horse and give you some food and refreshments before you leave."

"Thank you Sir," Gary said.

At the mother ship the Naproxian surveillance ship landed onto the landing deck. Upon going inside the pilot went to the Grand General of the mother ship. "May tech huway goola dash," the pilot said. [It looks like we have found an Earth colony.]

"Copae, Copae who muk tay?" asked the General.

[Good, Good how big of a find?]

"Sowa, Ku nida dash," said the pilot.

[Lots, they are scattered.]

"Ma kot lay me soya neck yup," ordered the General.

[In a few days we will send a prison ship.]

Christians were organizing for the upcoming invasion. The graduates from the peaceful school were waiting with: 'the cross bow' and 'the bow and arrow' and 'the sword and shield' fitted onto their sides and back. They were ready, however, they did not know when or where the attack would take place.

"Sup na net goola nash," said Nit.

[I can see the Earth colony.]

"Up may gonga hep," said Nit

[Let's land in front of those gates.]

Jeff looked up from 'peaceful school' and saw the prison ship hover over the school. Everybody, also looked up and saw it.

"Look! Look!" they yelled.

"Everybody take on your battle positions!" Jeff took command.

The school was full of graduates from the past five years. All they could do now was wait and respond to their circumstances.

The ship landed 20 yards from 'peaceful school' in front of their giant gates. A door electronically opened up and ten troops marched out holding spear like objects that gave out a zap like a lazer. "Ku bo dike nea put?" said the leader.

[Let's zap open these gates.]

Within a couple of moments the Naproxians opened up the gates. As they entered the gates, it seemed as though no body was there.

"Cuck nop de Zex eden," commanded the leader.

[Check out every room!]

The first room the soldiers went into was the bell tower and they saw Ernie crouched in a corner. Ernie looked at them remembering as to how they murdered his parents. His face was full of anger and fear. The three soldiers looked at the fat bald man as being helpless. The Naproxians put on their language converters thightly on to their mouths, "Come with us!" ordered the Naproxian leader.

"If you do not do as you are told, human, you will then become an example for the others!"

At that Ernie took his sword and swung it vertically at the wrist of the leader. Upon impact, he cut the leader's hand off at the wrist. The other Naproxians pointed their spears at Ernie, as they did a laser beam shot out of the tips of their spears. Ernie dropped his sword and shield and as he was dying, this last words were, "God help us at the hour of our need!" He gasped.

The Naproxians dragged Ernie's dead body into the middle of the court yard, "let this be an example to any human that resists capture!!" Second Commander yelled.

The Naproxians left the body laying there, then walked into the sleeping quarters and found the 13 year old children. They arrested 4 of them as well as Jill, the program co-ordinators. Everyone else in the sleeping quarters was silent as the Naproxians left with the prisoners, "Don't resist in any way or your fate will be like the fat man!" a Naproxian ordered.

The five of the prisoners were loaded onto the prisoner ship. The leader's wrist was taken care of by the Naproxian doctor.

"Got mare sak Genmic Sorel?" the doctor asked.

[What happened to you General?]

"Mot gok ne human," he answered.

[Attack by stupid human!]

"Lu mit pa lat ne gram," the doctor said.

[This artificial hand will operate soon.]

Meanwhile, the five prisoners, were put into the holding room. The three girls were scared and crying. The boy and Jill did not show any emotions but they felt 'fear' within themselves. Once the prisoners were left alone Jill told the children to bow down their heads in prayer.

"Dear heavenly Father, Lord of all creation, will you send down your Holy Spirit to watch over the kids and me as we have been captured by the

Naproxians, Amen"

The children felt better after Jill said the prayer. The ship started up its engines and left to a new location in order to land and pick up supplies such as water.

Chapter 5

The 'prisoner ship' surveyed the area for a place to land. When they saw the 'Valley of passion,' they concluded to land beside it since it was just 20 yards from a creek and all the green plants to pick for food.

Back in Westmore Land, Heather was at home with her parents and Chaldra. Heather felt bored that mid afternoon and decided to go on a trip to the church both to pray and for something to do, "I am going to the church," Heather told her parents.

"Be careful dear, with those damn Naproxians roaming about," warned John.

Heather wore all her 'war zone' gear in order to be safe just in case she ran into a Naproxian. You never know what the future holds she reasoned to herself.

After she prayed that God would protect mother, father, Chaldra and all the humans from the Naproxians, she went outside the church and ran into a man named Odin.

Smiling more than the Heavenly Father would bide him, Odin recomposed himself, looked at this mystic lady, and saw more than his senses could comprehend, what he saw was a Christian warrior woman in plain attire. He had to get to know her on a personal basis, to feel like a gentleman as he took her to a dance. Yet he promised God that he would not violate this special and mysterious creature he was confronted with.

Odin was thinking only the bible cherished the thought of the unicorn, and wise men thought of unicorns in order to remember the times before the flood, the way Heather looked she was, indeed, like a unicorn, because she was so unordinary.

Odin started to chuckle as he stared at Heather. Heather smiled back at Odin. Then shivers went down Odin's spine as he imagined her dressed in royal attire. It may be a better idea to treat her ordinary he thought.

Rex, a merchand from Ireland, watched Odin and Heather looking at each other. Odin, the son of a wealthy artist and Heather, a princess. He knew both of her parents and it was more than possible that they would make a perfect match. He knew that Heather excelled at peaceful school, and would make a perfect wife for any man.

Nearby, Oda, a priest of sorcery, felt both fear and hope when he looked into his crystal ball. He observed a war thousands of years ago between the ancestors before they signed a peace treaty. If these two were to get married it would put the worlds at peace except for the menace of the Naproxians. Oda had an itch and scratched it. Then Oda and Rex looked at each other, nodded and Oda closed his eyes in awe. Upon opening his eye, he put his long lonely cloak on and headed in the direction of the setting sun.

After walking a 100 yards, he yelled at Rex, "LOVE STRUCK!" Odin then introduced himself to Heather, "Hi, my name is Odin."

"Hi, I'm Heather."

"It's almost dark. May I escort you home?"

Heather blushed a little, Odin reminded her of her father. "Well sure," she said.

As they were traveling horse by horse, Odin reached over and took ahold of Heather's hand and Heather gripped his hand and she felt her heart beat. Heather had never been so confused about her feelings for a man.

When they reached the cabin, darkness was upon them. What would she tell her parents? She hoped her parents would like Odin.

"Would you like to meet my folks?" Heather asked as she dismounted her horse.

"Why not?" Odin replied.

"Well come in then," Heather responded.

Odin felt a bit nervous as they entered the cabin. Not because he was afraid but he just didn't know what to expect.

"Hi mom, hi dad, hi Chaldra, this is Odin. He escorted me home. I met him at the church," Heather explained.

Heather's mom looked at the strong, young well built man, reminding her of John when he was 20. The she looked at Heather and could not help but think of herself at 18. As she studied Heather's smile she sensed that this reunion was more than just an escort home. Oh wee, she must understand that Heather was a woman now, and it looked as though she had met a fine young man.

"Hi Odin, it is a pleasure to meet you," said Grace.

John looked at Okin and Heather and thought to himself that Heather had good taste. Although he wanted to get to know more about Odin. "Are you of Christian origin son?" John asked Odin.

"Yes sir of the Lutheran Christian family," Odin replied.

"I am going to need some help scrubbing down my horses. If we get you a blanket, will you stay the night?" John asked. "Besides, it's dangerous traveling at night with those damn Naproxians."

"Oh Please stay," Heather interrupted.

"I will stay only if we can give my horse a good cleaning too," Odin replied.

"Certainly!" Said John. "I am getting old and some young strong arms would be appreciated."

Grace went into the closet and took out a big thick blanket and gave it to Odin. Odin took the blanket and smiled at Grace.

"Odin you sleep in Chaldra's room, and Chaldra will sleep in the living room beside Heather," Grace said. "Is that okay with you Chaldra?"

"Not a problem at all."

As they all got ready for bed, John gave Odin an extra set of his bedtime wear. "Here, put these on and then come to the table for bed time prayer," John ordered Odin.

"Yes sir."

After everyone had their night time wear on and sat down at the table, John said a prayer, "Dear God, we thank you for our guest and would be most obliged, that if he can spare the time, we would treat him like family if he would stay awhile until the Naproxians leave. I also bless everyone within our cabin and ask you to keep them safe from harm. In the Lord's name...Amen."

After the prayer was over, Grace blew out the candle, everyone hugged and said goodnight and went to bed. Everyone slept peaceful except Heather who was confused regarding her feelings for Odin, and she tossed in her sleep a bit and woke up several times during the night.

The next morning Grace got up first and prepared porridge for breakfast. After they all ate, John and Okin filled a basin outside with water, stripped down the horses and started scrubbing them down.

"What type of work do your folks do son?" John asked.

"My father is an artist, and my mother is an herbal nurse."

"Odin is your last name 'Nork?'" asked John, "and your father Doug?"

"Why yes said Odin, how did you know that?"

"Because I remember seeing some of his paintings within our church," replied John.

"He enjoys doing that sort of thing and he taught me the trade also," Odin remarked. "Would you mind me painting a picture of Heather?"

"You're quite fond of her Odin?"

"Yes sir. She is not only unique, but she is beautiful."

Inside Grace and Heather stood by the window watching the men wash the horses.

"Not only is he handsome, but he sort of looks like Dad," Heather said. "I had a hard time sleeping last night mother."

At first her mother just stared at her daughter. Then she remembered when she was falling in love with John. If only her daughter was 2 again. Yet we all grow up, grow old and go back to the Father.

"It's okay dear, after all, it's the first time we had a guest in our cabin."

"But it's more than that mom, it's as if my feelings are all mixed up when I think of Odin," Heather explained.

"Tonight before bed, I will make you some herbal tea that will help you relax and have a good sleep," her mother counseled.

As a matter of fact, Grace understood as to what her daughter wanted, she desired to know Odin on a biological basis. Her mother also knew it was best for her to wait until she was married. That way the love of God would make it that more special. Yes, indeed, Grace remembered her first time making love to John. Heather watched Odin finish washing the horses with John.

After the horses were clean, the men put the riding gear back on the horses. Then they washed their hands and faces in the water basin. As they entered back into the cabin, they took their boots off and Odin still had his sleeves rolled up to his biceps. John gave Grace a hug and Odin looked at heather and John broke the moment.

"Give her a hug Odin," John said.

Heather ran over to Odin and gave him a hug just like Mom did to Dad and Odin gently put his arms around her shoulders for a full minute. Then Odin looked at John and Grace.

"You have a beautiful daughter," he said to them.

"You are a fine young man too," Grace replied.

"We raised her in every good way possible," John remarked.

Back at the valley of Passion, the Naproxians were gathering greens and collecting water.

"Ya soot ja nuba cat!" Said the General

[Make the humans move a little faster]

Lex put on his universal translating unit on to his lizard like mouth and talked directly to Jill, "You and the little units move faster or you will be punished!" said Lex, the gathering chief.

"We are not units. We are gentle human beings," Jill snapped.

The 'gathering chief' took a tool from the left side of his hip and he stuck it on Jill's hip.

'Zap' 'Zap' as it electronically shocked her.

"Ouch! That bloody well hurt," replied Jill.

"No more talking back human. Just gather water!" said Lex.

Jill, Susan, Matt, Alex and Dennis were covered in sweat and exhausted. They were ordered to make 500 trips to gather buckets of water from the creek and several trips to collect eatable plants for the Naproxian diet. All the while they were closely guarded.

"My feet and hands ache and I am so tired," said Susan.

Susan was a short 13 year old girl with blond hair, cute dimples and baby blue eyes and was very petite. Her little hands had blisters on them and her little body had not been worked so hard in her life.

"Don't complain too much out loud," Jill warned. "Or you might be punished."

"I will try not to complain," said little Susan.

Jill, Matt, Alex and Dennis were starting to feel very hungry. At that moment the Naproxians brought blue food cubes into 'the holding quarters,' however the cubes had no taste.

"Humans eat! This is your nourishment!" Said a female Naproxian. "My name is Nuke, and I feed our pet slaves."

Nuke seemed or was a little more friendly than other Naproxians. She studied 'human unit' at an academy on her planet, Naproxian. She had the opportunity to get close to one of her human subjects. She was quite close to him and named him, Zak. She also published a paper called, "So Chuck humans ye yap." It was all about adopting a human for either a pet or slave and the proper care for them.

Jill, Susan, Matt, Alex, and Dennis were so tired and desired some sleep. It seemed that the say was finished then Dennis spoke up, "They won't break me. I have a mind like a steel trap!" Dennis said bravely.

"You may need a mind like that!" Exclaimed Jill. "All of you come close to me for bed time prayer." "Now I lay me down to sleep. I pray the Lord my soul to keep. If I should die before I wake, then take my soul for heaven's sake!" "Amen"

Everybody cuddled up together and fell asleep. God had heard their prayer, and covered them all up with the Holy Spirit.

The Commander, Zeluk, announced that a council meeting would take place immediately at the Chambers. All the Naproxians were to attend.

"Qui les met du monts, " Zeluk told the crew.

[We will stay at this location for two months.]

"Nap tu ye humans got such!" Zeluk ordered.

[We will scan the area in twos to capture more humans slaves!]

"Tis nap me sut copete!" Zeluk said.

[This meeting is now complete and over.]

The next day, the Naproxians lined up outside of the ship and broke up in pairs, in order to survey the area for possible human slaves.

They were sent North, South, East, West, Southeast and Southwest. They were armed with a steel like suit and chains and a laser spear. However, they traveled by foot and were not fast walkers.

Jill, Susan, Matt, Alex and Dennis did not have to fetch water and greens today. They were given duties within the ship. These duties included: washing dishes, cleaning the walls and floors, giving baths and serving napox (a Naprosian spirit 'drink').

Nuke has a small daughter and Susan was Nuke's choice to give her a bath. While Susan was bathing Jet, Jet made a remark in Naproxian, "Mona dot human let salit?" Jet asked her Mom.

[Does human have germs Mommy?]

"human got worm it sat," answered Nuke.

[The human has been disinfected and is wearing gloves.

Jill's job was both to water the plants and was

the walls. It was not all that difficult water the plants, but washing the walls was a though job.

Dennis had to wash the dishes, Alex had to wash the floors and Max had an easy job serving Napox.

Depending on the conditions, they all worked throughout the day and were told these would be their basic duties. But that additional duties would be included if there was no work.

One of the Naproxian surveillance teams approcked Westmore land after walking for three days. They were approaching the cabin of John, Grace, Chaldra, Heather and Odin.

"Lite my human nichy," said Grone.

[Looks like a human dwelling.]

"Tis nock simplex gon do," said Nir.

[This should be an easy capture]

John, Grace, Chaldra, Heather, and Odin were about to eat and John started to say Supper prayers, "Dear Heavenly Father, we give thanks for the meal we are about to eat and we ask your protection during these dangerous times regarding the Naproxian invasion."

Crone accidently stepped into an empty bucked and kicked it off. The bucket hit John's horse and the horse made a loud noise.

"Why did the horse neigh?" asked Odin as he grabbed his sword and shield.

Heather jumped up and grabbed her cross bow.

John went into the bedroom and uncovered his cross bow from a box. Grace and Chaldra were ordered to stay in the bedroom by John.

In the next instance, the front door was kicked open by Crone. The two Naproxians entered the cabin and put their Universal Translators onto their mouths.

"Do not resist, you will be taken prisoner by the Naproxian Supreme Order," said Crone.

"Like Hell!" said Odin standing in front of everyone with sword and shield.

Crane lifted up and aimed his deadly spear in

order to kill Odin. But Odin quickly his behind his shield and the blast was reflected. Odin gripped his sword in his right hand and in a clean stroke, cut off Crane's head. The body and head fell to the dirt floor.

While Odin was looking at the remains of Crane, Nir aimed his spear at Odin's back. Heather saw Nirs intention and carefully aimed her cross bow at Nir's neck.

"Over here you lizard bastard!" yelled Heather.

Nir turned his head a moment to look at Heather. As his head turned, Heather released the arrow. Within a second, it entered into Nir's neck and Nir fell to his death.

Everyone grasped for a breath of air. Then they looked at the reptilian bodies.

"Odin and I will burn the bodies, fix the door and Heather, you watch Mom and Chaldra!" John ordered.

John and Odin burned the bodies and fixed the door the best they could. Then when all were together again, it felt very good to be alive.

"Okay everyone, it's getting late. Let's all get ready for bed," John said.

After changing, John said a special prayer to God before sleep, "Heavenly Father of all Creation, forgive us for killing two of your creatures, but it was necessary in order to protect us. May a peace treaty one day take place between the Naproxians and the humans. I say this in hope, Amen."

Everyone went to bed as Heather blew out the last candle. During the night both John and Grace woke up at the same time. "Are you awake Grace?" asked John.

"Yes," said Grace.

"I had a dream of what it was like on Naproxian before Aoraster ships rescued us and took us to Earth," said John.

"I had the same dream remembering working in those dirty mines," whispered Grace. "It was horrible."

"Best we get back to sleep," comforted John.

"Goodnight dear."

"Goodnight."

At base, the Naproxians woner shy Nir and Crane never reported their location.

"Lu neigh Zuk Nir sup Crane?" Zeluk asked, as he used his walkie talkie like instrument.

[Do you hear me Nir and Crane?]

At the cabin, everyone was having lunch. Chaldra prepared some chicken sandwiches and a glass of milk each.

"The Naproxians must have a home base nearby," Odin said.

"And they must have prisoners by now," John added. "Maybe I will go fetch Rex and we will get some men from 'peaceful school' and search for their home base."

"Then I guess I will stay here and guard the women," Odin replied.

"I will be gone 3 to 4 days and you and Heather must be ready for anything," John warned.

Grace got the message and packed up some of John's belongings and some food for the mission. John prepared his horse, strapped his belongings on to it and headed over to Rex's after mounting his horse. "Take care everyone, and I will be back in about 4 days," John said. "Odin, you and Heather watch out for Chaldra and Grace."

John waved a good bye for now. As he headed toward Rex's all he could think about was their safety. Rex lived close to Minister Right. It may be thoughtful to stop for a coffee with him too, John thought. John rode his horse at a fast trot as he headed toward Minister Right.

Chapter 6

    With Grace and Chaldra safe with Odin and Heather, John would contact Rex after having a coffee with Minister Right. He was sickened, both in heart and mind, disturbed beyond anything he had hoped would not happen on Earth, a Naproxian invasion.

    The horse he had rode at such a fast pace for a long time needed a rest. Only a few more minutes and they could take a rest and drink by a creek. The horse was sweating and panting, and when they arrived at the creek it was a good time to take a rest. Although the rest of the way was only two hours about one had to respect his horse.

    His first concern was finding enough men to locate the Naproxian home base. Without fear, John dismounted his horse and led her to the creek. She put her head into the water as John reached down and scooped up water splashing it on her. "There girl, There girl!" he said.

    "Lucy," he whispered, wanting to communicate with his horse needing to show her some respect. "You have been a good stallion for seven years girl."

    "Those Naproxians, those merciless lizards. I should have known, but I did suspect, they would find us sooner or later," John thought as he and Lucy refreshed themselves at the creek.

    After about ½ an hour, John put the reins back on Lucy and finished the trip to Minister Right.

    He knocked at the minister's door. "What do you say to brewing us a coffee Minster Right?"

    "I don't mind at all Sir John," he replied sadly. "I know what has happened John. We should be glad that we are still free. They are probably all around us by now. Come in, we should have a coffee."

    "Yes, you're right," John said, with a grim look on his face. He sadly told the minister about the two Naproxians that kicked down their door. For years there had been such peace within this land. Until now. Together they would all face this terrifying invasion. It was, at least, their right to give them the best we have.

John set down his coffee. "Sitting idle, we are like sitting ducks waiting to be shot, until they choose to attack us." Minister Right nodded, looking up at John with old green eyes.

"Be careful John, their weapons are more advanced than ours, but I think we out number them." He looked at John and John felt assured that the humans would some how win the war.

"Thank you for coffee," he said sincerely. "Thank you for your time, but I confess I think you should give me a prayer of yours."

"There is something about you John that is so sincere, bow your head."

"Yes Sir."

"Dear Heavenly Father, let your Holy Spirit protect and guide John and Rex as they gather forces to combat the Naproxians. I say this in your name. Amen."

"Thanks minister, we will give it our best, at any rate. Assured with your prayer, I am off to get Rex."

"I confess I have faith that God is with you son, and remember that I will be praying for your protection on your mission every day. I understand that you will need him."

John had enjoyed the time he had spent with Minister Right. He must consider that with God's help, the odds were more in his favour. He remembered 'That if one has faith as small as a mustard see, one can move a mountain.' It seemed, however, that defeating a race as advanced as the Naproxians would take more than just moving a mountain. He was only a few yards from Rex's place. Upon arrival he dismounted Lucy and went over to Rex's cabin and knocked on the door. "I will be honest with you Rex, I am not here for peaceful drinks."

"What is on your mind, John?"

"You are about ready to go on an important mission. You best invite me in to explain the details."

Rex sensed that this meeting regarded the Naproxians. Yes, or John would not have been so serious, and he realized that something must be done regarding them. "I would dare make a guess that this visit regards the Naproxians, well come in and talk."

John took off his boots and Rex told him to take a seat at the table. After they sat down, John began to speak, "You are aware of our new enemy?"

"I know who you are referring to, John. I have no wish to become one of their slaves."

John thought about that statement and agreed with him 100%. This thought of being a slave to lizards caused him to treat this meeting in a very serious way. "Can you travel with me to 'peaceful school' to gather up some men in order to find the Naproxian base?"

"You're damn right I can, when do you desire to leave?"

"As soon as possible, they already have troops out in Westmore Land, we had no choice but to kill two of them that tried to take us prisoners."

"I didn't know they would have soldiers out so soon!"

"They would have caught us unarmed if it would not have been that they spooked a horse that let out a 'neigh.' I guess the horse betrayed them.

Rex understood far too well the importance of getting a Christian army together. Not just two men, but a minimum of ten trained warriors and even then they had to be careful not to be detected.

"Heather has met a fine young man named Odin."

"Is it serious? Do you suppose they might marry?" Rex asked.

"My daughter seems to be quite in love with him," he answered happily. Yes, he knew eventually he would have to give Odin permission to marry Heather.

"You seem to respect Odin. I know his father, the artist, quite well. He is very wealthy and has many people that respect him."

"His name is Doug isn't it?"

"Yes, and his paintings are in many churches and school."

John grinned as he thought of Odin asking his permission to paint a picture of Heather. He wondered if Odin could paint as good as his father could. Having an artist in the family pleased John very well.

"Where are Odin and Heather now?"

"Back at the cabin watching over Grace and Chaldra," said John. "Odin is not only strong, but he is a very good warrior."

"Oh, a painter and a warrior, sounds like he is gentle and strong."

"I am very glad you approve of Odin."

Rex rose and asked John if he was ready to start the journey to 'peaceful school' tonight or not. "I think we should get a fresh start in the morning if you can supply me with a blanket for the night?"

"I can and besides, we don't want to travel in the dark."

"I know that you are right about that. We will get a fresh start first thing tomorrow morning."

When Rex and John had something to eat, they talked a while, then went to bed. Rex slept within his bedroom and John slept in the small guest room. John thought about Odin, Heather, Grace, and Chaldra and said a prayer for them before falling asleep, "Dear Heavenly Father, protect Odin, Heather, Grace and Chaldra and may you Holy Spirit be with Rex and I on our pilgrimage to peaceful school."

Back at John's cabin, before going to bed. Filled with a lot of love and respect Grace, Chaldra and Heather hugged each other and Odin, but just before bed, Grace asked Heather to say bed time prayer. Then, in a soft voice, she said, "Now I lay me down to sleep. I pray the Lord my soul to keep. If I shall die before I wake then take my soul for heaven's sake. Amen."

So, the next morning at sunrise, John and Rex woke up and dressed. Rex packed some food and belongings for the trip to 'peaceful school.' These men, both trained in Christian warfare, had to protect the human race. John stood by his horse with cross bow, bow and arrows, and his sword and shield, either at his side, or on his back. Rex was armed in a similar manner.

Filled with fear and hope, they mounted their horses and left the domain of Rex. They wanted to travel as far as possible during day light and sleep at night.

They welcomed the warm weather with a slight breeze. Their horses rode side by side except on trials that only allowed them to ride in single file. John's hands were ready for any sign of Naproxians. He had his left hand on the reins and his right hand by his sword and shield.

He told Rex aobut his experiences on Naproxian. He scared him a bit, for an instant Rex imagined being a prisoner himself. Then, quite brave, he touched his cross bow with confidence within himself as he looked at John with his hand on his sword and shield and quite confident, within himself.

"Ready for anything," he said to John as he stroked the neck of his horse. "I think I am also ready for any surprise attack." ...Two brave men.

A free, momentary experience riding side by side in such beautiful country. With such a good feeling being along side by side Mother Nature, they responded as though the Naproxians didn't exist. The Holy Spirit filled both of them up with love.

They would find the Naproxian home base in a couple of days when they arrived at the 'Valley of Passion.'

For the time they were safe, John was content as he steered his horse along the broken trial. He remembered the first time he and Heather traveled together.

He thought about Grace, Heather and Chaldra for a moment.

"What if those Naproxians raid our cabin again? Odin would have his hands full, one man, designated to protect them."

"Don't worry so much," Rex said, thinking not of anything possibly happening. He would have talked John into turning back if he had felt any danger, as he would have for his own daughter, if he had one. No, if any Naproxians raided John's cabin, Odin would take them on, and from what he heard of Heather, she was quite able to take care of herself. "Everything should be safe, John."

They picked up their pace a little as they passed a mountain and a creek. "We should take a little break by the creek and water the horses," John said.

"Sure sounds like a good idea."

They turned their horses toward the creek, once there, they dismounted the horses and guided them to the water to drink. "Look at the tracks in the mud, bigger than human feet," Rex said.

"That means either Naproxians have passed us or they have come here and went back to their home base," John said.

John and Rex observed the tracks closely and noticed they came to a stop then turned around. They could only conclude that they arrived here, turned around and then went back.

"We must be getting close to their home base," John said.

Rex studied the tracks. "Looks like about two days old."

What was that look in John's eyes? Was it something he said, or what John was looking at? "Quiet!" John ordered. Just down the creek was a Naproxian. Did he see them? No! They slowly guided their horses away from the creek into the woods without being detected. If only the horses would be quiet. "We had better get the hell out of here. There may be more of them!" John whispered.

"I agree."

They quietly moved their horses within the woods in order to hide themselves from any Naproxian soldiers. "We should be safe in those trees," John whispered.

They watched the Naproxians drink water and eat leafed plants. There in the water, three of them ate and drank. They led the horses as quietly and as far as possible away from them without being detected. After they led the horses a safe distance away, they mounted them and made their way taking a route around the enemy.

They felt anything but safe, and knew the threat was real. "Thank God we were not detected today; tonight we had better sleep without a fire," Rex suggested. It would be dangerous for them to have a fire, on the basis, that if they were close to the Naproxian home base they might be detected. It would be for their safety.

"No fire," John agreed.

"Then we might get a little cold but it will be worth it."

"My daughter has some close friends at 'peaceful school.' She will be eager to see them again." His heart went out to his daughter and the woman she was made into at 'peaceful school' and by him and Grace.

Rex looked at John and saw in him a resemblance to Odin. "Your daughter has picked a man after her father."

"Thank you." Oh, I guess as he remembered when he was a young warrior before he met Grace. It is a strange thing the way a daughter chooses a man like her dad. Or perhaps it is a subconscious thing. Surely then she would grow up to be as good of a wife to Odin as Grace has been to him. Except, of course, Grace never attended 'the war zone' at 'peaceful school.' Grace was a virgin when they were married and so was he, but he did not know for sure about Odin. Yet he was quite positive that Odin was a virgin too.

"Do you know if Odin is a virgin?" John asked.

"His father Doug would not have it any other way!" Rex assured.

"Heather is a virgin also."

"That's good. The first time will be blessed by God then."

"You have no idea how important that was to Grace. She would not have a man in any other way."

"Most Christians, including myself, reserve sex until they are married."

It was getting late and they were getting tired. The air was a bit cold, but the blankets would keep them warm enough.

"Let's call it a night," John said.

"We should say a brief prayer John."

"Okay, you say it."

Rex was quiet a second while he thought of the words. He remembered the days events, "Dear Heavenly Father, thank you for being there when we escaped detection from the enemy and bless John's family and the rest of us from the serious threat of the Naproxians. Amen."

After the prayer, both men wrapped themselves up in their blankets and fell asleep.

They traveled the next two days without any incidents. As they approached the Valley of Passion:

"Out of Hell itself!" John exclaimed as he surveyed around the valley and saw the Naproxian home base. There was a giant space craft with some Naproxian soldiers standing outside it. The ship was silver, round and glimmered in the sun. Vapors of steam come out of the middle of it.

Beside John, Rex whispered a brief prayer. His heart thumped as he imagined being captured, he felt disturbed by what they had found.

"We will have to ride around them without being detected, those soldiers are large and we could not handle them alone," John explained.

"We certainly could not!" agreed Rex.

"Should we go east and then circle back around to 'peaceful school?'" asked Rex.

"You are good in these woods." John thought about the old trails east. They were a little more rugged and would take a day longer. "Let's not waste time, and let's get out of here before a damn soldier spots us!"

"You lead the way John. We're off!"

"Okay!"

They took the long way around the 'Valley of Passion' in order to get to 'peaceful school.' It was quite a difficult and rugged journey. But they finally arrived at 'peaceful school' and they saw that the giant gates had to be repaired.

"We come from Westmore Land with news about the Naproxians!" John yelled through the message hole.

Minister Wise heard the yell and walked over to the gates and opened them.

"Welcome my friends," Minister Wise greeted them.

"We have found the Naproxian home base," John informed the minister.

"Where did you find it?"

"On the way here we ran into it at the 'Valley of Passion,'" Rex answered.

"How many of them are there?" asked Minister Wise.

"I don't know for sure," John said with his head bowed down in grief. "There is a whole ship of the bastards!"

The minister felt a little frightened. "They killed Ernie, the bell ringer, and we kept our distance and watched as they put Ernie's dead body on display in the middle of the court yard."

"Why didn't you kill them?" John asked.

"Because they had landed their damn ship a few yards from us and we didn't want a damn war here with the children," Minister Wise explained.

John reasoned that Minister Wise was right that a war would not be a good thing to expose 13 year olds to.

Chapter 7

After having morning breakfast, ignoring the Naproxian invasion, Chaldra went out into the woods alone to pick wild strawberries. She expected Grace to be more against her going out alone.

"I will be back in a couple of hours," Chaldra said.

"Have fun picking strawberries and be careful," Odin said.

Going down on her knees, she was amazed at the amount of wild strawberries there were. Not wishing to sound noisy, she did not talk nor sing to herself while she worked. She was only certain that she had wandered an hour away form home.

So she proceeded in silence, until her bucket was full.

"Do not move nor speak," Mila, a Naproxian soldier said.

Chaldra turned her head and standing in front of her stood a giant lizard man in armor. With his universal translator on, he took away her strawberries, set them down and put chains around her hands.

"Have you seen any other people like us?" she asked.

"No I have not!" Chanldra answered.

"You are now the property of the Naproxian order!" Mila, the soldier, said. "Do not try to escape!"

Mila then took out the chains from her side and bound Chaldra's wrists and said, "you will come with me!"

She followed Mila as she led her away from 'Westmore Land' to the Naproxian home base. She, not wishing to take a chance on looking for his lost soldiers, was happy with her catch. Chaldra was not sure how to react, and was only certain that she was scared as she followed Mila the Naproxian soldier.

So they proceeded away, until it became dark. "I will chain you to the tree until morning," Mila told Chaldra.

It was not comfortable sleeping chained to a

tree. "This is not going to be a comfortable sleep!" Chaldra complained.

"Quiet or I will tighten the chains on you," Mila replied. Her tone was like a machine. She was content with her catch. The high commander would be proud of her when they arrived at home base. She would be rewarded with a special Naproxian drink, for his catch. She would make a good maid Milo thought. She was not affected by the fact that Chaldra was tied in chains to a tree.

"It has been hours and we have not see Chaldra," Grace said to Odin and Heather. "We simply cannot leave her out in the woods all night. What if she has lost her way?"

"Chaldra knows how to survive in a situation where she has to spend a night alone in the woods?" Odin asked. "It may not be a good idea to risk the rest of us to go looking for her at this hour."

"You're right of course. Chaldra is more than trained to take care of herself for one night," Grace assured. "We must look for her first thing tomorrow morning."

"You mean we simply leave her alone over the night?" Heather asked.

"It's simply too dangerous for us to start searching for her at this hour both because of the Naproxians and because we don't also want to get lost in the woods." Grace explained to Heather. "It is always better to be wise rather than foolish."

They all got into their night wear. It would not be an easy sleep tonight without Chaldra. If only she would come walking into the cabin, Heather thought. That would have been the ideal solution. Before the three of them finally went to bed, Grace said she would say the evening prayer, "Dear God, please watch over Chaldra wherever she may be and also please look out for John and Rex on their mission to put together a Christian army and please also watch over us. I say this in the Lord's name. Amen."

They all hugged and then they went to bed. As they slept they slept restlessly thinking of Chaldra. Heather wake up a couple of times in horror imaging what may have happened to Chaldra. Then she fell back asleep until the morning.

In the morning the first one that woke up was Odin. He woke up the rest of them reminding them that a search party had to be organized to search for their lost member.

"I think it is the best for me to go in full armor to look for Chaldra," Odin said. "And Heather you wear full armor and look out for Grace just in case the Naproxians pay you a visit!"

"You take care of yourself Odin and I will watch out for mom!" Heather reassured.

Odin changed into his day clothing and fully armed himself with every weapon. He ate breakfast with Grace and Heather and then he was ready to go out into the woods in order to find their lost Chaldra.

"We will be seeing you women in a while after I find the where abouts of Chaldra." Odin said as he closed the cabin door. "Make sure you women lock the door!" Odin ordered.

Odin saw the track of Chaldra and followed them to the best of his ability. Upon following her tracks, he came across a second set of tracks and identified them to himself as Naproxian footwear. "Shit!" he said to himself. "Chaldra is a prisoner and I better get back to Heather and Grace since they may need my protection Odin murmured to himself.

Upon arriving at the cabin, Odin took in a deep breath before he gave Heather and Grace the news.

"Chaldra has been captured!" Odin said after Heather let him into the cabin. "I didn't follow the tracks just in case one or two of them found their way to the cabin. I came back as soon as I could!" Odin expressed.

"My God!" Heather expressed. "My dear Chaldra captured by those damn Naproxians."

"I am very horrified and sad at the bad news." Grace expressed.

"I think our best bet is to wait for John and Rex to organize a Christian army." Odin said. "I am sure they will find the Naproxians home base and rescue Chaldra and any others they may have captured."

Chapter 8

John stood in the middle of the court yard at 'peaceful school.' The members both old and new stood around him. The old man had eyes of experience. The audience put the full faith in him as he addressed them.

"As you know, we have all been invaded by a race referred to as the Naproxian order." John said. "In order to defeat them we must organize ourselves and attack their home base." As John spoke, dread flooded through peaceful school.

He said the older members must wear full armor and that some of them must play the role as guardians over the young ones. "The rest of us must make a plan of attack on the Naproxian home base located at the Valley of Passion. We discovered it on our way here.

John took a stick and drew a map in the dirt and pointed out the exact whereabouts of the Naproxian ship. Then he devised a plan as to the best method they would use in the attack. "I think we should surround the ship from the rear, so they are unaware of us, then as a team sneak around to the front of the ship and catch them by surprise!" John surmised.

And that was what the plan was and it was hoped that no one would be captured or condemned to death. More plans would have to be made for cases of unexpected things. Nevertheless, the basic idea was to catch them by surprise.

John looked all the Christian soldiers who had proven themselves at 'peaceful school.' "Jeff and Rex, can you both help me organize everyone into four groups. One to look after the old and children and three to attack the Naproxian home base?" John said in a warm voice.

There were no questions. Could it be that John was accepted as wise and their leader right away. He was very wise regarding the Naproxians because he had dealt with them before. He looked at all the eyes looking at him. "Okay everyone make a circle around me," he ordered.

After all the Christian men, women and children made a circle around him, John began to speak. "I was confronted with the Naproxian when I was a young man. Although they have superior strength and technology, they do have a few weaknesses that we encountered with them. Their biggest weakness is that they are robot like, logical and do not have an imagination. The second weakness they have is that they are attached to their young." Everybody listened in silence as John spoke to them. "so let's break up into 4 teams and then let's do some planning as to the best method of attack and rescue!"

Everybody, except the children, counted around the circle 1 to 4 and then broke up into 4 even groups. John ordered the different groups to each find a spot and wait for further orders. The groups each found a spot within the court yard and each group waited for John to come over and devise his wise plans.

Chapter 9

At the Naproxian home base, Mila arrived with Chaldra.

"Su lee nick human chowing beana."

[I caught this human picking berries.]

The General's looked at Chaldra and upon studying her age excetra decided that she would make a fine maid.

"Tu la human at le servey clack" the General ordered.

[Take this human and dress her in a maid's clothing.]

Chaldra did not understand what they were talking about at first then Mila put on her 'universal translator' looked at Chaldra and began to speak, "Come with me to our women to change your clothing into maid's wear and they will train you for your duties," ordered Mila.

"I don't want to be a maid to damn lizards!" Chaldra screamed.

"Maybe a zap from my spear will change your attitude?"

"That will not be necessary, please lead the way," Chaldra conformed.

They went into the space ship and Mila led her to a giant laundry facility, full of dirty clothing and bed-time blankets.

"The ladies will teach you how to do laundry and then you will learn your other duties!" Mila ordered.

The laundry machines were huge and the room had a lizard odor to them. Chaldra thought to herself that the job would not be half bad if it was not for the stinking smell. Oh well, at least she was alive and possibly the Christian army would rescue her soon? The female Naproxians all put on the 'universal translators' and began to instruct Chaldra.

"You must always wash the men's clothing in this machine," Cupid said and taught Chaldra how to run it. "And the female clothing in this machine!"

Chaldra did not have any problems learning

how to use the washing machines. She did not like the job, but thanked God that she was as lucky as she presently was. The lizard smell at first made her feel like getting sick. Lizard sweat glands gave off a worse odor than humans. The clothing was also larger than human clothing and quite heavy. The lizard women kept on eye on her for the first few hours then left her to do the work by herself.

"Work hard and I will show you your other duties once the laundry is done!" Cupid said as she came into check on Chaldra. "Make sure you don't mix the men's clothing up with the women's!"

"Ne pick de human seta my nock," the General ordered.

[Get a human search team together!"

There was a quick response. Could the lizards capture more humans? The General did not think of loading up his ship with humans and then going back to Naproxia, justifiably, that was his intention. He organized three groups of warriors, but he had to think of a location to search for humans next.

At 'peaceful school' they were armed and ready to invade the Naproxian home base. That would mean that some of the Naproxian warriors would have left the ship to search for humans which would give the Christian soldiers a little bit of an advantage. But, the Christian soldiers did not know they would have that advantage only if they attacked the Naproxian home base before the lizard soldiers came back.

Chapter 10

Heather was alone with Grace as they waiter together for John, Odin and the Christian Army. Grace seemed to be unsettled, and although she was extremely confident in John's abilities, she would not relax until this Naproxian invasion was over and finished with. As far as she was concerned, she and her 'Royal' family were more important than those damn lizards.

Not that she considered herself better than any Christians. Even, thinking, a beggar was no less of a person so long as they had a giant Christian heart. Although she came from noble birth, she did not push it on anybody. So completely loving was she. Now, here in this beautiful country, the sun up and the wind blowing briskly, it did not seem so bad that she was the Queen of Zoraster and her daughter her princess.

"You will all have our family as your King, Queen, and princess again," she reminded herself. She had hoped that it would not have come to a war to make people realize the importance of leadership. She looked at Heather, now a full grown princess, for she had given birth to only one child, she was her pride and joy.

The Christian soldiers were planning their attack on the Naproxian home base tomorrow. The would go across the old bridge of great strength, leading to the path to the 'Valley of Passion.' With twilight rapidly falling, the air was cool and the scent of flowers drifted about them. In front of John the troops were given words of encouragement. Swans flew over peaceful school, perhaps, a sign from God that they were going to have good luck.

John drew in a deep breath. He looked at all his soldiers and he hoped that none of them would lose their lives. Although he knew that maybe an absurd wish. In the event that we lose a few good men, at least let's hope, we can retrieve the, give them a proper burial and hope the lizards do not do experiments on their bodies.

Rex came over to John and put his hand on

his shoulder and looked at his face. "What is wrong John?" I realize the Naproxians are huge and have advanced technology, but surely we out number them."

"I just remembered facing this lizard race before ad they are good in battle," John replied.

"Naturally I expect you to be a little afraid, but I also expect you to lead us to victory!"

John was silent a moment. "I will do the best of my God given ability in order to lead us to Victory...you have my word!"

John looked at his Christian army with pride. They had all been trained at 'peaceful school' and were all experts at the cross bow, the sword and shield, and the bow and arrow. It hurt that some of them would loose their lives in battle with the Naproxians, but at least, for sure, their souls would go to heaven and join their old ancestors. We are all ready for battle John thought to himself!

"Rex?" John asked, standing with both hands by his side, standing in an erect position and with a few tears rolling down his cheeks.

"What's up John?" Rex asked.

"Help me go to everyone and let them know we are at war as of tomorrow morning!" John wiped the last tear from his cheek. "It is best to let each person know, on a personal basis; now get busy. Twilight is just about upon us."

"Okay John. I will start informing each warrior on a personal basis." Rex complied.

The both started going to each individual man, woman and child and let them know to get ready for tomorrow, because we are at war with the Naproxians. "I am no suggesting you are insane John, but how do we stand a chance? I am simply saying they are an advanced race and have advanced technology. What will happen to us in battle?" Susan asked.

"An arrow through the heart, or the blade of a sword across the neck will even kill a lizard," John assured.

After everyone was informed and had their

'war zone' gear together, Minister Wise announced that everyone should go into 'the eatery' for a special service. Everyone filled up 'the eatery.' Some were sitting and some were standing. Minister Wise found his way to the front of everyone. "Everyone bow your heads. Heavenly God, as of tomorrow these brave men and women will be confronting an evil adversary. It is a race of lizard people who have fallen away from you. May your Holy Spirit be upon them and protect them!! Amen."

After the prayer, all the men, women and children went to bed and slept until the sun rose in the purple sky.

Chapter 11

As the sun was now shining in the Western sky, the new bell ringer went over to the bell tower. He was also a short man like Ernie used to be. However, he was of a slight build. He wrapped his skinny short finger around the bell rope, and Eddie pulled the rope three times: Dong! Dong! Dong!

Everyone within 'peaceful school' go out of bed, dressed and headed toward 'the eatery.' It was the first time the whole eatery was full. They lined up for eggs, bacon, ham and toast. Before they ate, Minister Wise walked toward the front. On the way, we hugged several people and said, "God Bless," to them. When he passed by Odin he inquired: "Young man, I have never met you before. I am Minister Wise."

"I am Odin, Son of the artist, Doug Asped from the Christian clan to the West. I came here with John in order to help you with the war efforts against the Naproxians."

"I wish you the best of luck and God's blessing."

The minister was now in front of everyone.

"Today, before you go to war, I will say the Lord's prayer as grace. Our Father, who art in heaven, hallowed be thy name. Thy Kingdom come, thy will be done on Earth as it is in heaven. As this day our daily bread and forgive my trespasses as I forgive those who trespass against me. Lead me not into temptation, but deliver me from evil. For thine is the Kingdom, the power and the glory. For ever and ever, amen. Enjoy your breakfast and after you have done, I wish all of you my blessings as you go out to battle the Naproxians," finished Minister Wise.

As to the war, everyone felt both a tinge of fear, but each was also blessed with the Holy Spirit.

Just before they left the large gate, they saw a Naproxian woman running toward the gate holding a white piece of cloth. "Don't shoot, don't shoot. I come in peace and speak English!!"

She was carrying a medium sized steel box

with English writings on it. She was a large lizard, although it still looked as if the box was quite heavy. She arrived at the front gates. "Don't be afraid, I am on the side of humans. I joined their cause on Zoraster. When the humans were used on Naproxia, I had some human slaves and we became friends. I was trained to be a spy. And in order to make a long story short, I am looking for a man named John from Westmore land.

"John this lady claims she needs to talk to you!" said Minister Wise.

"What may I do for you?" asked John.

"I smuggled this radio equipment for you from the special agents on Zoraster to give you in the case that the Naproxians invaded Earth."

"John took the steel box, opened up the lid of the box and found light speed transmission radios.

"With this equipment, we will be able to radio for help within a week from Zoraster," said John. "God gives his blessings in the strangest of ways!"

Just before leaving and leading the Christian troops into battle, he handed the equipment to Minister Wise and told him to put it in a very safe hiding place, until they returned.

"No one will find it!" said Minister Wise.

The lizard lady began to speak to the Christian soldiers in an informed way, "The General of the Naproxian ship has sent out three armies, in order to catch more human slaves as of this morning," Yetyat told them. "I had better head back to the Naproxian ship before they miss me."

Chapter 12

Although Heather's parent had enjoyed the beauty of Zoraster before they were kidnapped in a Naproxian invasion and sold as slaves, Heather never had a chance to see her world. The prospect of finally seeing a world full of trees, flowers, ponds, three suns and two moons appealed to her. Their cities were built near huge mountains reaching onto the mountains and spreading into the valleys and trees below. Many of these cities looked like a dream of heaven. Everyone had plenty of wealth because there was so much to go around.

Although some of the cities had technology, built space craft, most people were happy to live with the bare necessities. Heather could only imagine Zoraster from what her mother and father told her about it. For the last couple of years, Heather wondered what it would be like to meet other men and women that were the same as her.

It could be that Grace understood Heather's desire to have friends that were like her, because, at times Grace also missed socializing with the same species. Although a war was starting here, on Earth, the Christians against the Naproxians, things were different on both Zoraster and Naproxia. The leaders were in the middle of a diplomatic mission to create and sign a peace treaty.

"We have been at war for 100 years," The Grand Ambassador Cecil said. "If we sign a peace treaty, share our resources and become friends, then that would make us both more happy and at peace."

The lizard dictator thought over what Cecil said and replied, after putting on his Universal Translator, "You humans have taught us a lot about love. Not only have some of us intermarried, but we now have half lizard and half human babies on both planets. You may make up a contract for a 'peace treaty' between our worlds, and we will comply, read it over and sign it. You have also shown us that you are equal to us in battle and it would seem logical to have us as an ally.

The dictator, Zu Nick, made arrangements to meet with Cecil on Wednesday and today was Tuesday. The meeting would be held on a Naproxian military base on 'platene' at 9:00am sharp. Zu Nick told Cecil to have all the peace treaty contracts with him and to come alone.

Unlike the dictator, Zu Nick, who would not have trusted Cecil, Cecil agreed that a peace treaty would be signed at 9:00am sharp on Wednesday and that he would take a one many ship to platene.

All that night, without sleep, Cecil worked on making up a 'peace treaty' in both English and Naproxian. It was 7:00am and Cecil just finished the final drafts. He estimated it would take on hour and 45 minutes traveling at 6 knots per second to reach platene. He loaded the contracts into his briefcase and headed to the military moon of platene. The planet was surrounded by armoured ships. Then an escort ship arrived beside Cecil's ship and John put on his screen.

"Follow me to our leader's private chambers Cecil." The pilot said. "Zu Nick is expecting you. We are not at peace yet, so watch your step!"

"Okay, lead the way and I will follow you," Cecil complied.

They both passed a number of different patrol ships and then flew into a large crater to a landing deck. They landed their ships in order…Zu Nick then Cecil.

Cecil stayed in his ship until Zu Nick walked over then Cecil lowered his door.

"Do no move any further," Zu Nick said. "You will be escorted by guards for your safety."

Two large Naproxian guards; one on Cecil's left and the other on his right.

"Act as though you are a prisoner then you will be safe!" Zu Nick advised.

There was a touch of humour when Cecil finally came to the Chambers of Lister (The Lizard Dictator).

"So you want us to become allies ambassador?" Lister studied Cecil closely for any sign of dishonesty. "It would do us both good to be allies. Together we could rule the Universe and share our recourses. All hunger would disappear and we would have a chance to share cultures."

"Yes, I think it would be a wise move for both of our species and the Universe at large!" replied Cecil.

Lister thought it over carefully and also thought about all the human slaves he would have to set free if he agreed to the peace treaty, "Let me read over the peace treaty then!" Lister ordered.

A young boy went over to Cecil, took the peace treaty contract over to Lister. Lister read the treaty out loud, sat silent for a second and the nodded his head, "Okay Cecil, you may come to the bench and we will sign the treaties," Lister said.

Cecil walked over to the bench and both of them signed the treaty. Now after years of fighting, killing and controlling 'the Universe' was at peace.

Thank God, all human slaves would either be set free or be treated with respect and salary where they did their work. It was almost noon by the time the peace treaty was complete, but how long could we keep the peace. If anything, some traitor may act in such a way as to start the war all over again. The might have, if it was not for the fact that we all die and that leaders change during our life times and other things, made the peace treaty forever.

Outside, as Zu Nick announced over a loud speaker that the war is over and all human slaves are now free, you could hear everyone yelling and clapping. Humans could be heard louder than the lizards, "We're free! We're free! We're free!"

Chapter 13

As the Christian army moved in closer to the 'Naproxian base' they, being prepared for battle, and they were very surprised at what they saw. Jill, Susan, Matt, Alex and Dennis were all outside with lizard children playing catch with a ball.

The Christian army could not believe their eyes. What is going on? Lizard children playing catch with human children. Not only were the children playing but the adult lizards were clapping their hands. Every Christian soldier turned their eyes toward John.

"Okay, I will go over to the ship and see what's going on!" John said. "You all wait here until I get back."

Something does not seem logical. Am I going crazy or what? John thought as he walked toward the ship. Upon getting within talking distance John began to speak, "What the hell is going on here? Why are lizards and humans playing together?"

A large lizard put on his 'Universal Translator" and went over to John. His name was Crone.

"Our supreme leader has informed us that a peace treaty has been signed between the lizards and the humans. We are at peace," Crone informed John."

"So that's why you are clapping hands and the children are playing?" John asked.

"Yes, of course, because now we are one big family," Crone said.

"May I take Chaldra, Jill and the children with me then?" John asked.

"Of course!" Crone answered.

John walked over to Chaldra first and gave her a great big hug. Her hair was down, she was dressed up like a maid and her eyes looked tired. Holding back her shoulders, she looked into John's eyes and began to cry.

"Are you okay? Did they treat you very badly?" John asked.

"I had to work in a smelly laundry room, until

a lizard named Zuback told me that I was free to go, on the basis, we are now free."

"I don't want to hear anymore about the laundry room. Let's gather up the kids and head back to 'peaceful school' and let them know the good news." John said. "You hear me, Chaldra?"

Chaldra went over to Jill first. "John said we should gather up the kids to bring them back to 'peaceful school.'"

So Chaldra and Jill walked over to the kids. They stopped for a moment and were filled with a sense of happiness as they watched the little lizard boys and girls playing catch with Susan, Matt, Alex, and Dennis. Dennis seemed to be getting along quite well with a lizard boy named, Diter.

"Come children, John is waiting for us and we must get back to 'peaceful school.'

"Can Diter come with us for awhile?" asked Dennis who felt affection for the lizard boy.

"Well, Jill we are at peace now," said Chaldra.

"We will have to check with his parents in order to find out if it is okay," answered Jill.

Jill and Chaldra told John what Dennis wanted and he approved. Meanwhile the Christian army was getting impatient.

"We will take Susan, Matt and Alex to the wood and you, Jill and Dennis go check with Diter's mom and see what you can work out," said John.

When Jill and Chaldra finally found Diter's parents, they were quite surprised at their response. They made arrangements for Diter no only to stay at 'peaceful school' for a year but to stay for the entire program if he so desired. Dennis was very happy and could not wait to get to know him better. They all joined the Christian solders in the woods. While the other children would go back to Naproxia, Diter would be the first lizard to attend 'peaceful school.' He could learn Christianity, weapons, games and really get to know human beings. Now, that they arrived back to 'peaceful school' they would have to announce that a peace treaty has been signed and that they are no longer at war.

John went over to Minister Wise, told him the war is over and asked for the radio equipment given to him by the Naproxian spy.

"Minister Wise could you please get me the radio equipment so that I may contact my old ship commander Ben?" John asked.

"You certainly may, I have it stored away in my office," Minister Wise explained.

Then both Minister Wise and John walked over to the office in order to get the radio equipment. John took two hours setting up all the equipment. Then he decided to try it out. If I can remember Ben's damn radio codes, I should be able to reach him. John thought to himself. Now let's remember, DA DA 9913. Yes that's it now all I have to do is punch in the code and I should be able to broad cast the code into space and contact my old friend Ben.

"DADA9913…DADA9913…DADA9913"

"This is Ben, who have I the opportunity to speak with? I have not used this code in many years!" Ben said.

"It's John from the Earth colony established 20 years ago during the Naproxian invasion, do you copy?" asked John.

"John! John! Old friend and captain. How the hell are you doing? How are Heather and Grace?"

"Heather is a lady now, and Grace is just doing fine. I heard that finally a 'peace treaty' has been signed between Zoraster and Naproxian. Could it be true?"

"Yes, John, at last after 100 years, the galaxy and Universe are at peace!" Ben explained.

John took in a deep breath, he found it hard to believe, but he saw it with his own eyes. Naproxian children and human children palying ball in front of the Naproxian space ship.

"John we are going to send Zoraster ships to Earth in order to celebrate this special occasion, and also, make you, Grace and Heather…King, Queen and Princess once more over the whole universe!" Ben explained.

"One second Ben, I think that there is going to

be a prince too. Heather has fallen in love with a good young Christian man with the name Odin." John explained.

"I see. Well we should arrive at Earth in a week at light speed. Let's hope for the best, over and out."

"Over and out Ben."

Chapter 13

Odin and John are at 'peaceful school' talking man to man. "John, I have a very personal question to ask you." He took in a breath. "Is it okay?" asked Odin.

"Well, of course, what's up?" asked John.

"You see sir, I love your daughter, Heather, very much and I am asking your permission to have her as my bride?"

John looked and realized as to how much Odin resembled himself when he was a young man. Then he looked deep into Odin's eyes as a tear of hope rolled down Odin's cheek. Odin would be a great son in law, he thought, and he would make a fine prince.

"Son, if you treat my daughter like a princess, then you have my permission to have her as your bride." John replied.

"Thank you sir, her treatment will be 100% to my ability." Odin assured. "Let's find Rex, the merchant, so that I can buy her an engagement ring."

"I saw him with the boys playing with Diter, the lizard boy, at the 'games room'" John said.

"Great, and thanks again sir!" Odin said with pride.

Odin walked swiftly over to the 'games room' to get a hold of Rex. Upon finding him, he asked Rex for a few minutes of his time. Rex did not mind.

"What's up Odin?" Rex asked when they were alone in the court yard.

"I would love to buy an engagement ring off you my friendly merchant." Odin asked.

"I bet I know whom the lucky woman is." Rex assured.

"Who then?"

"It must be Heather."

"Yes, and I love her with my full heart!" Odin confirmed. "I want the best engagement ring you have!"

"Well" Rex agreed. "How would you like to buy a little gem I have with diamonds resembling a unicorn's head?"

"Let's see it?" Odin asked.

Rex walked over to his supply wagon and opened a special box up that contained the ring and walked back to Odin. He showed him the ring.

"Heather will love the choice of this ring!" Rex exclaimed.

"That is the most perfect ring for Heather." Odin whispered. "I will buy it!"

They both settled business regarding the engagement ring. It was very expensive but Odin did not mind. Afterwards he went over to John to show him the ring.

"Sir, I picked out an engagement ring for Heather," Odin told him.

"Let's see if boy!" John ordered.

Odin put his hand into his pocket, took out the ring and showed it to John.

"See, John it is in the shape of a Unicorn's head."

John looked at it and observed the gold and diamonds shaped in such a way as to resemble a Unicorn's head and he knew it must have been expensive.

"Fantastic taste Odin. Heather will love it!" John exclaimed.

As they looked eye to eye, a feeling crept through John, as he would be losing his baby girl. But he could not have given her away to a better man. Odin resembled himself in so many ways he thought to himself.

"We had better get back to our women and give them the good news about the peace treaty!" John ordered.

Odin wanted to get back too, but for different reasons.

"We're off." Said Odin.

They walked together toward their horses, passing by Minister Wise, and let him know that they were heading back to Westmore land. Odin quickly mounted his horse but John took a bit longer both missed the women a lot.

Four days later the cabin was in view.

"Finally made it boy." John said. "They have been alone for two weeks."

"I hope they don't miss Chaldra that much." Odin remarked.

Chapter 14

"How you women doing?" John moved past Odin and took off his boots.

"We are doing okay. How are you and Odin?" Grace asked.

"We had a long trip back from 'peaceful school.' Take my cloak Heather." She walked over to her dad, held the cloak in one arm and gave him a hug with the other.

"I am so glad to see you dad, and you too Odin. Please let me give Odin a hug dad?"

"Go ahead Heather?"

She wrapped her arms around Odin's neck and snuggled her face close to his. Her body was tight against his. Odin put his arms gently around Heather's waist.

Their feelings toward each other were obvious to Grace. They let go of each other and Odin took off his boots and also handed his cloak to Heather. She went over to the closet and hung up the cloaks. She is beautiful, Odin thought quietly to himself.

Grace looked at John with a confused look on her face.

"What's wrong Grace?"

"In all the excitement, I forgot about Chaldra?" asked Grace.

"Don't worry about her, she is safe at 'peaceful school.'" John assured.

Grace gave a sign of relief. She too in a deep breath the let it out. The thought of the Naproxians filled her mind. What if something sinister happened to Chaldra. She tried to hold back her fear. She put on a phony smile so nobody would suspect that she was concerned. If John, Odin or Heather knew she was frightened, it would only serve to get them upset. What Grace did not know yet was that humans and Naproxians had signed a peace treaty. If she knew, she would have felt at ease. It will be a blessing to her when John or Odin tell her the story about the peace treaty.

"I'll see that we get some more meat in here. I

will kill a couple of chickens tomorrow." John said.

"I put the axe in the closet. You will need it to kill the chickens tomorrow. I'll put it by the back door John," Grace instructed.

Odin looked over at Heather with a gleam within his eyes. "You want to go for a walk with me Heather?"

"Now?" A confused look came over Heather. "It is very dark and cold outside."

Odin looked outside, and then agreed that it could wait until tomorrow.

"You're right Heather. It is kind of late to go for a walk." Odin shrugged.

John told everyone that he and Odin had a story to tell them. While John told the story about the peace treaty with the Naproxians, Grace boiled up some water on the stove and served everyone some herb tea. She kept her ears alert and heard the entire story. The tea was sweet from the honey suckles and after drinking it, everyone felt quite tired. As you looked outside from the window, the full moon radiated in the summer sky.

"Good night" they all said to each other as they got ready for bed.

"Oh, before you fall asleep, let me say the Lord's Prayer." Grace ordered.

They were all in agreement. "Our Father who art in heaven, hallowed be thy name. Our kingdom come. Thy will be done on Earth as it is in heaven. Forgive my trespasses as I forgive those who trespass against me, and lead me not into temptation, but deliver me from evil. For thine is the kingdom, the power, and the glory, for ever and ever...amen."

Aware the God's spirit was with them, they all fell fast asleep.

While they were sleeping, Odin dreamed about giving Heather her engagement ring. He dreamt that she would accept it then he would ask her if she would get married to him. Then he stared for an answer, but she did not answer him in the dream. He would have to wait for the answer until tomorrow.

Tomorrow came soon enough. Before you

knew it, like a sunflower, the sun was boldly rising in the east. But Odin was not the first one up. Grace was. She made everyone bacon, eggs and toast then called them for breakfast. Still in night wear, they all came to the table for breakfast.

"God bless the meal we are about to receive." Said John.

A few minutes into the meal, Odin reminded Heather about going for a walk. She looked at him with her big doe eyes and said, "Okay, Odin, as long as we get home before lunch." She joked.

"It will be sooner than you think," assured Odin.

"I will kill a couple of chickens while you kids are gone," said John.

"John?" Grace said. "I'll still have to get you the axe. I forgot to put it by the door."

She went to the closet to fetch the axe and to her surprise, it was gone. "I thought I put it here. Where could it have gone?"

"Is somebody looking for my axe?" asked John as he held it up.

"I beat you to it Grace."

"Is there anything else you need dear?"

"Nope, nothing," he said, then he went out the door with the axe in his hand.

"He is always a step ahead of me Heather."

In the kitchen, Odin helped Heather with the dishes, while Grace worked at putting the blankets away.

"Are we going to walk on the trail to the church?" Heather asked.

Then Odin thought that if they took the horses to the church, Minister Right could bless their engagement.

"Let's take the horses Heather. It will be a nice ride and we can stop and see Minister Right?"

"Sounds like fun."

Odin put on his boots and Heather put on her shoes. They told Grace they would be home for lunch. Then they mounted their horses and headed over to the church.

"Isn't this beautiful country?" Odin asked.

"Yes, it is, and I would love to live here for the rest of my life."

They passed many trees, green plants and colorful wild flowers. Just ahead of them was the church.

Odin said, "Heather let's stop here for a few minutes. I have something to ask you."

"Sure Odin."

"Well, can you please get off your horse for a minute?"

Heather and Odin dismounted their horses. Heather was concerned. Had she done something wrong? Why, all of a sudden was Odin so serious?

"Heather?"

"Yes, Odin?"

"Well, Heather, I have something very, well important, well serious to ask you."

"What Odin?"

"You see Heather, from the first time I saw you, I fell in love with you and in my pocket I have something for you."

"Well get it out of your pocket Odin!"

Odin put his hand into his pocket and took out the engagement ring. Then he took Heather's hand and said, "Heather, with this ring, I promise to love you for the rest of my life and I ask you with all of my heart to be my wife one day?"

Heather's face turned pink, then her eyes started to burn, then a few tears ran down her cheek. After wiping them off, she replied to Odin, "I love you too. I accept this engagement ring and I will become you wife Odin." She said in a state of shock. "Odin, dear Odin, this is one of the happiest moments of my life." She said as she adjusted the ring.

They both stood there staring at each other for a couple of moments. The moved their bodies in close, put their arms around each other. Then as if God made them do it, their lips met and they felt strange as they kissed. The both wanted more, but Heather said, "Wait Odin, let's not go any further until after we are married. We can wait Odin. It will be that much more special," Heather explained.

"I have waited this long, I can wait until we're married," agreed Odin.

The looked into each other's eyes and knew how beautiful it would be to become one. But they could wait because with God's blessing it would mean so much more!

"Let's go over to Minister Right's and give him the good news," Odin suggested. As he looked at Heather, he noticed that she had such an innocent smile on her face that he could not help loving her. The gathered up their horses and walked toward the Minister's house holding hands with one hand, and guiding their horses by the reins with the other.

About 100 meters away stood the house of the Minister. The sun was now in the middle of the blue sky and beat down on them both. Heather's face was blushed a little red from the sun. As they stood in front of the Minister's house, after tying up their horses to a weeping willow tree, Odin knocked on the door. Within a few moments, Minister Right opened the door.

"What a surprise. Odin and Heather, what can I do for you today?"

"Well," Odin said, "you see, Heather and I just got engaged, and we wanted your blessing."

The minister looked at young, tall and strong Odin, then looked at tall, dignified and remarkably beautiful, Heather. They do make a great pair and both come from very good parents. But did Odin realize that Heather was secretly a princess. Anyway, they made a very good match as far as he was concerned.

"Come in, come in. We will have a tea and then I will pray for God's blessing to be upon you both," insisted Minister Right.

"Thank you sir," Odin said.

Odin took off his boots and Heather removed her shoes. As they entered the Minister's house, Odin recognized a painting of 'The Last Supper' that his father had painted.

"How did you get that painting in your living

room Minister?" Odin asked.   He was sure he recognized it.

"Yes, it's one of my favorites.   Your father donated it to me as a gift, Odin, and he said that you were a very good artist yourself?"

"I am not bad.   My father taught me since I was 13 and I apprenticed with him while my friends almost all went to the 'peaceful school.'   Although I did some schooling, most of what I know I learned from my father."

"And I am sure he taught you to the best of his ability and very good," the Minister assured.

The three of them, then, sat down for tea.   The Minister made them a dandelion flower tea that was slightly sweet and a bit bitter.

"Would either of you like some sugar?" asked Minister Right.

"I will have a little," said Heather.

"No thank you," replied Odin.

The three of them chatted about Heather's parents, Odin's parents, and this and that for about an hour.   The covered quite a bit.   The only other good news to the Minister, besides their engagement, that surprised him, was the 'peace treaty' between human and Naproxian.   The Minister put their tea cups, respectively, into the washing basin and then told them to bow their heads for a blessing.   He put one of his hands on Heather's left shoulder, and his other hand on Odin's right shoulder.   "Dear Lord, as I rise up both Heather and Odin, I ask thee to bless their engagement in the name of the Father, the Son, and the Holy Spirit.   Wherever they go and as to which circumstances they may encounter may your blessing always be with them. Amen"

Heather and Odin felt the Holy Spirit within themselves.   Heather cried a little, gave the Minister a hug, looked at Odin and was one happy young lady.

Both went to the door and put on their foot wear.   Odin shook the Minister's hand and thanked him.   As they went outside they felt the mild wind upon them from the South and was actually quite comforting.   They mounted their horses, waved good-bye to the Minister, and headed home.

When they were home, her mother asked Heather as to how their visit was with Minister Right.

Heather said, "Mom he is such a wonder man. He gave me and Odin his blessing, and I was a wonderful painting of 'The Last Supper' done by Odin's father."

"I am so happy for you Heather," Grace said.

Chapter 15

"Nut go Zoraster ney Naproxian righ?" asked the General.

[Who will rule the people in this new treaty?]

"Way be nut go ney foe," replied the Head of Relations.

[We will have to have a meeting with the human senate.]

"Way be nut ney Zoraster," said 1st Relations Officer.

[The human Senate is in Bethule, a remote village on Zoraster.]

"Subit 'peaceful school' er mitake," ordered the General.

[Let the people in charge at 'Peaceful School' know our desires.]

At the General's command, a group of three Naproxians geared up to bring the request to Minister Wise at 'Peaceful School."

By this time, not only were the Naproxian and human children playing and having fun with each other but the adults were competing in archery and the sword and shield. All of 'peaceful school' was a combination of Naproxians and humans getting along for the first time in a thousand years.

The three Naproxians, ordered by the General to talk to Minister Wise, finally arrived at 'Peaceful School." Upon putting on their Universal translators, the first officer began to speak. "We are ordered by the General to talk to Minister Wise?" he said.

"Come with me and I will take you to him," a weary old lady named Beth said.

The three soldiers followed Beth to Minister Wise's office. She knocked on the door three times.

"Come in please," said Minister Wise. "How may I help you?"

"These three men have a message for you," Beth said.

"Okay, leave us alone and I will talk to them," said Minister Wise.

"Yes, gentlemen, what is on your mind?"

The leader of the group began to speak. "Our General thinks that now that the worlds are at peace, we must choose a divine leader as our sovereign," Jatoot explained.

Minister Wise thought the matter over and realized that a Senate meeting in Bethule on Zoraster was the human custom in these cases. He decided he would send some men to fetch John from Westmore land, since he knew the right radio codes and as to which person to talk to. "I will have to bring somebody else here before I can contact Zoraster." Minister Wise explained everything to the Naproxians. "Come back in six days."

The Naproxians shook their heads in agreement, took out a communicator and contacted the General. The General told them to stay at 'peaceful school' until they had some fee back from Bethule. The Naproxians explained the General's orders and John took them to show them where they would sleep.

"In the meantime, make yourselves at home, and take part in the activities," said Minister Wise.

Then Minister Wise sent two of his best men to Westmore land in order to get John. After a two day trip they arrived at John's cabin, went to the door and knocked. John opened the door, the men explained that Minister Wise sent them and John, therefore, invited them in. After taking off their boots, John invited them to talk at the table.

"The Naproxians think we should elect a leader now that humans and Naproxians are at peace and they desire a Senate meeting," Carlose explained. "Mr Wise wants you to contact Bethule on the transmitter regarding this matter."

John explained that they would all head to 'peaceful school' in the morning because now it was too dark out. Grace, Heather and Odin made room for the men to sleep and as usual Grace said a prayer, "Now I lay me down to sleep. I pray the Lord my soul to keep. If I should die before I wake, take my soul for heaven's sake. Amen."

The next morning, after they had all had breakfast, Odin, Heather and Grace, it was decided who would accompany the group back to 'peaceful school.'

Chapter 16

John, Odin, Heather and Grace and the two guides arrived safely to 'peaceful school' and were presently in Minister Wise's office with the three Naproxians. "This is John Storm calling from Earth code #128?229913, do you copy?" John asked into the radio transmitter.

A few moments later, John received a reply.

"Is that really you John? Long time no see. How the heck are you?" Ernie Diefenbas, the Senate head asked. "How may I assist you old pal?"

"We want to choose a Universal leader now that the Naproxians and the humans are at peace again," John replied.

"You know that your family has ruled for thousands of years John. Why should it be any different now?" Ernie asked. "Do you feel that you, Grace and Heather can fill the position again?"

"Of course we can, but the Naproxians have to agree, and they have asked for an election."

"That may not be the only way of having them agree to put your family in charge. Several worlds love your ancestry, and if we gather up enough planets, the Naproxians may agree with our intention," explained Ernie.

"Well get on to it then, and I will explain things on Earth to the Naproxian General and oh by the way, Heather is getting married to an A1 young many named Odin," said John.

"Congratulate her then on my behalf, and I will start contacting leaders to put you and your family of Royal Blood back in charge of the Universe. In the meantime, take care of everyone John!" Ernie explained.

It took several weeks for Ernie to contact the different leaders of the neighboring planets, but he managed to contact 9/9 of them, and they were all persuaded to vote John Storm's family back into Supreme Rulers of the Universe. The reasons that they chose John and family was because of their divine love for every living thing and because of their inborn sensitivity to every living thing, including plants and animals.

Even the Naproxians gave in when diplomats visited their leader and gave him evidence that 9/9 planets agreed that John Storm and family would represent the Universe better than anybody else.

Plans were being made to build a beautiful castle on Earth as to where John's family would rule the Universe from. Different planets could send space craft to them for Counsel in the times of need or for advise. All this was agreed upon by all of the leaders of the various planets, including, of course, Naproxian. Naproxian was last to sign the treaty, but since 9/9 planets had agreed that John Storm's family had done well in the past, and that they would in the future, the Naproxians signed the treaty. All of the planets within the known Universe helped both build the Royal Castle, and the runways for space craft to land. It, the castle and runways, were a combination of ancient technology and modern technology. The castle itself looked ancient, but the runways looked modern, or better yet, like the future.

The total building, of these head quarters, took five years. Both Odin and Heather agreed to save their marriage until the place was complete. At last, five years later, with the help of thousands, everything was finally finished and what a magnificent sight it was! Here John and family would rule in peace. Westmore land was the Pinnacle of the whole Universe.

Chapter 17

One autumn day, Heather now 24 years old and Odin 25 years old were both holding hand as they went for a walk. "Heather, we have been engaged for six years. Don't you feel we should finally get married?" Odin asked.

"Oh yes Odin, as soon as possible. Mom and Dad have already made up a Royal bedroom for us to use within their magnificent castle," Heather said with a smile.

"So, let's talk to our parents, and have a Royal wedding then Heather," confirmed Odin.

The two of them talked to both sides of their families and agree, on the date of the marriage. It would be May 1st. Everyday Heather and Odin went for a walk. Chaldra always packed them a lunch and May was coming up fast.

Plans were being made for the leaders of the nine planets and their dignitaries to attend the wedding. Everyone, both rich and poor on Earth were also invited. The day of the wedding was only a week away.

Heather and Odin found and hired Rex to fit them in both a wedding dress for Heather and a tuxedo for Odin. Rex, a man with grand taste sold his best to them as they deserved nothing but the best. Rex was one of Odin's choices as best man.

It seemed now that time was moving fast. The day of the wedding was finally here.

Chapter 18

Grace, John, Doug, and Carol all sat together on the balcony of the castle in the very middle of the wedding ceremony. The leaders of the nine planets all stood together in a line below the castle balcony. Everybody from Earth that attended stretched out a hundred yards long and a hundred yards wide. The wedding party all stood underneath the balcony also but ahead of their parents.

At the sound of a trumpet, Odin walked over by the wedding party to a spot in front of Minister Wise. Hen Heather walked over to her father and he took her hand and walked her from the balcony, down the stairs and over to Odin. She felt her heart beating fast as she stood beside Odin. This is the day she was waiting for. It was 5 whole years since they had become engaged and were blessed by Minister Right.

"We are gathered here on this special day in front of the Castle of John and Grace Storm in order to wed their daughter Heather to Odin in holy matrimony. If anyone objects, may we hear them now or forever hold your peace. Odin do you take Heather for better or for worse, for sickness and in health, forever to be your wife, so help you God? If so say, 'I do.'"

"I do," said Odin.

"And you Heather, do you take Odin for better or for worse, for sickness and in health to be your husband so help you God? If so say 'I do.'"

"I do," said Heather.

"Then in God's name I pronounce you both man and wife. Odin you may kiss the bride."

Odin put his head underneath Heather's veil, and gave her a giant and long kiss. Then the people laughed, and Heather helped out by putting her veil over her head and Odin kissed her again. Everybody clapped, fire works went off, and everyone cheered.

The leaders of the nine planets walked over and shook Odin's and Heather's hand. Then music and wine and food were served to everyone by the servants and helpers. Odin took Heather's hand and they departed into the Royal Bedroom that John and Grace prepared for them. Upon entering the bedroom and locking the door they were both standing by the bed.

"I don't want to hurt you," Odin said.

"Don't be silly Odin, I will be okay," Heather reassured.

Odin slowly undressed Heather until she was standing in the nude then he slowly undressed himself. Both stood in the nude looking at each other naked for the first time.

"It says in the bible that we should become one," said Odin.

"Yes, it does. Odin come closer," Heather whispered.

Odin moved in close until his body and Heather's were touching each other and he felt strange. He then became more aggressive and kissed Heather's neck and pulled her onto the bed. Heather succumbed to him, moaning as he made love to her. Their bodies for several moments became one. After it was over, Heather said, "That was beautiful Odin, and I love you very much."

"I didn't hurt you did I?" asked Odin with a worried look.

"Of course no silly, that's how God meant it to be," said Heather.

"Thank God," said Odin as he took in a couple of breaths.

The wedding was always remembered by Odin and Heather and the remained together and helped rule in peace for some years. Then one day, Heather seemed a little odd. She wasn't the same, and wanted to be left alone. Odin was worried by her rejection of him and her strange cravings for pickles.

"What's wrong with you?" he inquired.

"Odin, I think I'm pregnant," she said.

"You mean to say you're going to have a baby?" Odin asked.

"Yes Odin, I think so."

Odin's eyes widened. He could not believe

his ears. Soon he would be a father. Odin's chest was puffed up and he felt very proud. He, him, Odin...a father. Odin kept asking Heather, as the baby started to show on her, "Are you okay?" he kept asking.

"Don't move around too much. I will get you supper in bed," he would say.

Then nine months later the nurse called Odin to their Royal room, and said, "Odin, you are a father to a handsome little boy."

The End